KOPAL-KUNDALA

KOPAL-KUNDALA

A TALE OF BENGALI LIFE

BANKIM CHANDRA CHATTERJI
HENRY ARTHUR DEUTEROS PHILLIPS

GYAN

Published by

GYAN

Gyan Publishing House
5, Ansari Road
Daryaganj, New Delhi-110002
Phone: 011-47034999, 9811692060
E-mail: books@gyanbooks.com

Distribution Network
gyanbooks.com
India, USA, Canada, UK, Australia

ISBN: 978-93-7316-001-6 (PB)

First Published, 1885

2nd Impression 2025

Printed at: Gyan Press, Delhi.

KOPAL-KUNDALA
Arthur: BANKIM CHANDRA CHATTERJI
HENRY ARTHUR DEUTEROS PHILLIPS

KOPAL-KUNDALA.

KOPAL-KUNDALA:

A Tale of Bengali Life:

TRANSLATED FROM THE BENGALI OF BUNKIM CHANDRA CHATTERJEE

BY

H. A. D. PHILLIPS,

BENGAL CIVIL SERVICE,

SOMETIME SCHOLAR OF BRASENOSE COLLEGE, OXFORD.

1885.

TO MY UNCLE,

H. D. PHILLIPS, Esq., J.P.,

FORMERLY JUDGE OF THE HIGH COURT AND MEMBER OF THE GOVERNOR'S COUNCIL, MADRAS.

THIS VOLUME

IS

affectionately inscribed.

CONTENTS.

PART III.

PART IV.

INTRODUCTORY ESSAY ON BENGAL AND BENGALI NOVELISTS.

A KNOWLEDGE of the vernacular is necessary for all officials, while, in the case of judicial officers, it may be regarded as a *sine quâ non.* The magistrate, who is thoroughly at home in the language, is able to dispose of cases with promptitude, and feels a certainty as to the correctness of his decision which cannot be felt by those who have to rely, in whole or in part, on the services of an interpreter. These facts alone constitute a sufficient incentive for acquiring a complete mastery of the language. No doubt, speaking generally, the vernacular languages of India are not worth studying for the sake of their literature; but if in this respect one vernacular is worthy of study more than another, it is certainly the Bengali language.

Many people in England regard the natives of India much in the same light as they regard the natives of Africa. A perusal of the following tale will at least give them some conception of the stage of civilization at which the Bengali race has arrived, and of the intellectual attainments of the educated classes. A few words regarding the Province and its material progress may not be out of place.

The census of 1881 shows that the population, which now stands at 69,536,861, has increased 10·89 per cent. in ten years. The Hindus number 45,452,806, and the Mohammedans 21,704,724. The average density of persons to the square mile is 371·41. In some districts the average density of the *rural* population exceeds 1000 to the square mile, and has caused some alarm. Hitherto there have been no migratory movements on a large scale, owing to the conservative habits of the people and the fondness of the agricultural community for their ancestral fields and homesteads.

> "Beatus ille, qui procul negotiis
> Paterna rura bubus exercet suis."

But the danger, though appreciable, is not so great as is supposed. There are vast tracts of untenanted and untilled lands awaiting the plough, and these lands are in some cases situate within a few miles of those parts where the density of population is greatest. Emigration, though still unpopular, is losing its unpopularity by degrees. Education is spreading among the masses, and the old order is changing, giving place to new. That which has happened in western countries will assuredly happen in India. During the year 1882 nearly 11,000 persons were registered as emigrants for tea-gardens in Assam, and nearly 9000 were despatched to Mauritius, Trinidad, and other colonies. The fact that 2000 of these emigrants were Brahmans is a hopeful sign, and indicates that caste prejudices are dying away.

Cultivation is improving, and the fact that the land goes on producing good crops year after year seems to negative the supposition that the soil is being deteriorated or gradually exhausted. As to famine, alarmists should bear in mind the fact that India is a food-exporting country, and nothing short of general widespread famine could stop such exportation. In India the anxiety is not so much on account of the sufficiency of food-supplies as of the difficulty of transportation in emergencies to distressed areas; and, with the extension of railways, this difficulty is gradually disappearing.

The judicial system is most elaborate, and, in the case of the criminal courts at any rate, justice is not only exceedingly cheap, but brought to the doors of the people in a manner that is quite unknown in European countries. The jails and jail administration may compare favourably with European countries.

The number and value of civil suits has largely increased, while the number of notarial registrations in 1882–83 exceeded half a million. There is scarcely a branch of the administration which does not point to the increase and diffusion of wealth, and the material progress of the country. The Government has not only not enhanced the land revenue, but the rate of incidence per acre has actually been diminished. Nevertheless, owing to increased cultivation, the receipts from this source continue to rise in the temporarily settled provinces. In permanently settled Bengal the revenue paid by the Zemindars represents only three or four per cent. of the value of the gross produce. The receipts from salt, excise, stamps, forests, registration, post-offices, and telegraphs continue to rise. In another decade the excise revenue will probably rank in importance with the revenues from salt and opium.

The material progress and increased comfort of the people makes itself manifest in many ways. District officers are unanimous in their reports on this subject. More masonry houses are being built; substantial tanks and wells are excavated; orchards of fruit trees are being planted in large numbers; stone and earthenware vessels have given way to brass utensils; wooden bedsteads, chairs, and stools are to be seen in the houses of all but the very poorest classes. The number of carts for transport has increased by thousands, and the number of draught bullocks by tens of thousands. During the scarcity of 1874 nearly a quarter of a million draught bullocks were collected in a few weeks in Northern Behar and Bengal for the transport of grain by Government. On the rivers, too, the number of boats has largely increased, and they are of a better and more substantial kind. Nowadays the ryot may be seen tramping along with an umbrella in his hand, and, if the weather be fine, shoes on his feet; if wet or muddy, he generally carries his shoes in his hand or slings them across his shoulder! He wears better clothes, and covers the upper part of his body with a jacket or coat, while in the cold weather he has also a shawl or wrapper. The wages of labour have largely increased, and women of the lowest classes may be seen with silver ornaments; brass ornaments are giving way to silver and silver to gold. The quantity and quality of jewellery worn by the women is a very sure and safe criterion of the prosperity of the people, as it is notorious that they like to invest a great portion of their savings in this way. Thefts and housebreakings, and the occasional occurrence of dacoities or gang-robberies, show that the habit of hoarding and burying treasure is not yet extinct, and that the desire of the people, and especially of the trading classes, to conceal their wealth, is still prevalent, though not so strong as under native rule. Magistrates feel some surprise on reading the daily police reports of crime to find that sums of five hundred to a thousand rupees in cash and ornaments have been stolen from some oil-seller or cloth-seller who does not even pay the license tax! These facts are mentioned to show that the outward and visible signs of comfort and prosperity are not the only indications of the wealth of the country. Of course Indians, as compared with Europeans, are poor, and must remain so for a long time to come; but their wants in the shape of food, housing, and clothing, are smaller and more easily and cheaply satisfied. It is probable that the poorest classes feel the pinch of poverty far less than the same classes in England; hunger is not dreaded in ordinary times, nor are there any sufferings from the rigours of climate. The private charity shown towards the old, infirm, and helpless, as well as towards religious mendicants and professional beggars, has hitherto obviated the necessity for any poor law, and is one of the best elements of the native character. Dr. Birdwood ascribes the comfort and happiness of the agricultural classes to the happy administration of the land, and the excellent character of the landed tenures. Certainly the land question seems to have been solved in India in a satisfactory manner, while its solution is as yet incomplete in Ireland, and appears to be only beginning in England and Scotland.

Though wealth is still hoarded to some extent, the natives have become fully alive to the benefits of trade, commerce, and investment of capital. Twenty millions sterling of the national debt of India is held by natives; and the reason they do not hold more is that they can generally get safe investments, which yield more than 4 or 4½ per cent. Deposits in the Savings Banks are increasing, and the people are thoroughly familiar with currency notes, as is evident from the fact that during the year 1882–83 the total issues of notes from treasuries in Bengal amounted to £3,880,000, while the receipts of currency notes from the public amounted to £3,600,000. The increased enlightenment and prosperity of the people is manifest also from the postal and telegraphic transactions of the country. At the close of the year 1882–83 there were in the province of Bengal 1439 imperial post-offices and 3512 letter-boxes. The number of miles of lines open was 10,845 (exclusive of railway mileage). The number of articles of all kinds received for delivery during the same year was 41,829,892 as against 38,431,484 in the previous year, showing an increase of 8·8 per cent. The value of insured letters and parcels delivered by the post-office reached the high figure of £1,550,000. The rate of postage compares most favourably with that of European countries. For two pice (= three-farthings) a letter can be sent from Scinde to Assam, from Peshawur to Cape Comorin (nearly two thousand miles)! The postage from London to Brussels is twopence-halfpenny.[1]

[1] The above facts are worthy of the attention of persistent and pessimist detractors of Anglo-Indian administration, such as Messrs. Blunt, Hyndman, and Seymour Keay.

Professor Seeley, in his "Expansion of England," has shown that India has no nationality or national unity. The English did not introduce a foreign domination into India; the foreign domination was there already. Prior to British rule, lawless anarchy was the chronic state of the country from the time of the invasion of Mahmoud. Such anarchy was suspended for a short time over a portion only of Northern India during the reigns of Akber and Shah Jehan. With this exception it may be said that there never was any security for person or property, much less for trade and commerce. The Maharatta rule was but an organised system of robbery and pillage.

Under the English India is more united than she ever was before. But even so, there is no Indian nationality. There are different religions and different languages. Islam and Hinduism neutralise each other, and thereby create a sort of equilibrium. For eight hundred years before the advent of the British the Indians were under oppressive foreign despots; the British rule has at least been benevolent and humanising. After centuries of misrule and oppression the country is at rest and enjoying to the utmost the blessings of peace, order, and civilization.

As to the danger of foreign invasion, it may be said that India has from a remote period been swept from time to time by waves of invasion from beyond its north-west frontier. The white-skinned Aryans must themselves have been the first. Then comes Alexander the Great and the Scythian invasions; then in succession Mahmoud of Ghazni, Tamerlane, and Baber; and lastly, Nadir Shah and Ahmed Shah. But in those times there was no solidity in the empire such as there is at present; nor were there the same means of resistance. Moreover, an oppressed people, ground down with taxation, might naturally welcome a new ruler. But the keenest opponents of British rule know only too well that, by the advent of Russia, they would be jumping from the frying-pan into the fire. As for internal dangers, they can only become appreciable when we cease to govern India for India. At the same time we should not neglect the ordinary precautions which the strongest European Governments deem it necessary to take against disloyalty and sedition.

The foregoing sketch is of use in judging and accounting for the peculiar position and character of Bengali literature. A backward people have, so to speak, rushed to civilization at one bound; old customs and prejudices have been displaced, *uno ictu*, by a state of enlightenment and advanced ideas. The educated classes have suddenly found themselves face to face with the richest gems of western learning and literature. The clash of widely divergent stages of civilization, the juxtaposition of the most advanced thought with comparative barbarism has produced results which, though perhaps to be expected, are somewhat curious. If one tries to close a box packed with more than it can hold, the lid may be unhinged,—new wine may burst old bottles. The colliding forces of divergent stages of civilization have produced a literature that, for want of a better expression, may be called a hybrid compromise between eastern and western ideas. So we find that the Bengali novel is to a great extent an exotic. It is a hothouse plant which has been brought from a foreign soil; but even crude imitations are better than the farragos of original nonsense, lists of which appear from time to time in the pages of the *Calcutta Gazette*.

The above remarks are merely general, and there exist of course bright and notable exceptions, among whom may be mentioned the names of Peary Chund Mitter (the father of Bengali novelists), Bunkim Chandra Chatterji, Romesh Chandra Dutt, and Tarak Nath Ganguli. The "Allaler Gharer Dulal" of the first-mentioned author may be called a truly indigenous novel, in which some of the reigning vices and follies of the time are held up to scorn and derision. A deep vein of moral earnestness runs through all the writings of Peary Chund Mitter, and he takes the opportunity to interweave with the incidents of his story disquisitions on virtue and vice, truthfulness and deceit, charity and niggardliness, hypocrisy and straightforwardness. Not only general vices, such as drinking and debauchery, but particular customs, such as a kulin marrying a dozen wives and living at their expense, are condemned in no measured terms. The book is written in a plain colloquial style, which, combined with a quiet humour, procured for it a considerable degree of popularity. Towards the latter end of his life Peary Chund Mitter gave up novel-writing and wrote several pamphlets on religious subjects and short memoirs of eminent men, of which the "Life of David Hare" (first written in English and then translated into Bengali) is best known.

"Durgesa-Nandini" was the first novel written by Bunkim Chandra Chatterji.

Though he borrows to a great extent from English novelists he has too much originality to be a mere servile imitator. Some of his novels contain exceedingly realistic descriptions of domestic life; as, for instance, the mid-day scenes in the inner apartments of Jogendro Nath's house (Bisha-Brikhya). The Bengali language and literature are much indebted to this prolific writer. He has enlarged the capacity of the language for the expression of varied ideas, and has imparted to it a degree of elasticity which it did not before possess. The style is pithy, incisive, and elegant; while avoiding the stilted, pompous, and florid diction heretofore in vogue, he has improved on the simple but somewhat bald style of Peary Chund Mitter.

Romesh Chandra Dutt may be called the Sir Walter Scott of Bengal. His works embrace the period during which the Maharatta power was on the ascendant, and describe the marvellous perseverance and heroism of Sivaji. To my mind, the style and language are perfect. Lucid and perspicuous to a degree, there is a finish, a musical arrangement of cadence, and occasionally a richness of phrase that remind one of the rhythmical and rounded periods of Macaulay. Aspirant Bengali writers of novel or romance cannot do better than saturate themselves with the style of Romesh Chandra Dutt.

I believe Tarak Nath Ganguli has written one novel only, namely, "Sorna-Lota;" but this novel is truly indigenous. It describes the every-day life, the incidents, the cares, the quarrels, the intrigues of a Hindu joint family. There is room for plenty more novels of this sort. In a prose romance or novel, the first matter of interest is the scheme, the idea, the subject. Next come the incidents—on which depends the construction, the interest of the plot. Improbability of incident is generally resented by an educated reader; and such resentment is a wholesome critical feeling, though, if carried too far, there could be no prose fiction whatever but the novels of real life. Much of the interest of a novel depends, again, on the author's powers of description, whether of scenery or of every-day objects and places of social resort. But it is by his characters that a novelist is chiefly judged. Estimated according to these tests, "Sorna-Lota" takes a high place among Bengali novels.

It would exceed the limits and scope of this notice were I to mention all works deserving of mention. But I cannot refrain from naming Indronath Banerjee, Damodhur Mookerjee, and the talented authoress of "Dîp Nirbân." Indronath Banerjee's "Kolpa Toru" is a work of merit. In point of caustic humour he perhaps has no equal; and the pages of "Punchanonda" (Bengali *Punch*) contain some very witty and sparkling sketches from his pen.

A word of advice in conclusion to present and future writers. Society can only be improved by faithfully pourtraying it as it is, and showing up its worst phases. To conceal, to gloss over, to pretend that no cancers exist can only increase the virulence of the cancers. In order to excite loathing and contempt they must be held up in all their ugly nakedness. Shib Chandra Dutt, in "The Hindus as They Are," has made a very mild and tentative step in this direction; at least so it appears to those who are conversant with the biting lampoons and satires of English literature. Nevertheless, he has been abused by many of his countrymen for letting in the light of day on portions of the inner life of the people; but there is nothing that he has written which was not known to many European officers. A magistrate, perhaps, sees the worst side of the people; but the bad must be described along with the good; otherwise the picture is inaccurate and misleading. Prose fiction possesses advantages superior either to history or to poetry. It has been remarked that it is chiefly in the fictions of an age that we can discover the modes of living, dress, and manners of the period. In this respect, much remains for Bengali fiction writers. Let them describe the domestic and social life, the cities and villages, dwelling-houses, temples, shops, furniture, clothing and finery, jewellery, toilet requisites, dietary and utensils for preparation, the use of stimulants, opium, ganja, betel, drinks, &c. Again, under the head of morals and customs, may be mentioned descriptions of ceremonies, such as betrothals and marriages, pregnancy and births, death and burial, contracts and oaths, proverbs, sports and games, pictures, &c. Then there is agricultural life and the microcosm of the Bengali village, with its numerous members, the relations of landlords and tenants, litigation, money-lending and indebtedness, the various phases of crime as seen in the criminal courts, the peculiar position of prostitutes, the breaking up of joint life, the virtue and truly Christian self-denial of some widows, the laxity of others, the music and musical instruments, education, emigration, diseases, religion and religious customs, idols and their appurtenances, priests, female priests, astrologers, the police, the village police, the jails, dramatic representations, dancing, singing, recreations, and amusements,—these and a thousand other subjects may well be touched on in the novels of real life. I should be extremely glad if aspirant writers would take a hint from the above disjointed list, and produce some really indigenous novels that would be interesting not only to Indian but to English readers.

For the portion of this article that treats of the relative merits of various Bengali novelists I am indebted to some extent to my friend and *quondam* tutor Babu Krishna Kishor Acharjya, Sheristadar of the Thakbust Office, Midnapore.

H. A. D. PHILLIPS,
Bengal Civil Service.

E. I. U. S. CLUB, LONDON,
March 5, 1885.

KOPAL-KUNDALA.

PART I.

CHAPTER I.

AT THE MEETING OF THE WATERS.

At the end of a night in the month of Mágh [1] two hundred and fifty years ago a pilgrim-boat was returning from Gangá-ságor.[2] At that time it was the custom for boats to go in numbers together owing to dread of Portuguese pirates; but this boat was alone, as towards the end of night a dense fog had spread on every side, and the sailors, not know-

[1] The Bengali month of Mágh corresponds to one half of December and one half of January.

[2] Gangá-ságor, where the Ganges meets the sea, now known as Sangor Point and Lighthouse. A religious fair of great importance is annually held on the island of Sangor, which is a celebrated place of pilgrimage.

ing in what direction to steer, had wandered far from their proper course. Now there was no certainty whatever as to where they were going or in what direction. Nearly all the passengers were asleep: an old man and a young man were the only two awake. As they were conversing together, the old man suddenly stopped the conversation, and asked the sailors how far they would be able to go that day. One of the sailors, after humming and hawing a little, replied, "I cannot say."

The old man got angry, and began to reproach the sailor. The young man said—

"Sir, what is in God's hand the wisest men do not know, so how can that yokel tell you? Don't be fidgetty."

"Don't be fidgetty," testily replied the old man; "do you know the rascals have cut twenty or twenty-five bigahs of my paddy,[1]

[1] Paddy-cutting cases are very common in the police courts of Bengal. About 75 per cent. of all the litigation in Bengal relates to or arises out of disputes concerning land. It has been remarked that any fool can try a murder case, but it requires a born judge to unravel the merits of a paddy-cutting case.

and what are my children to eat for a whole year?"

This news he had received after coming to Ságor from other pilgrims who had subsequently arrived. The young man said—

"I told you before you ought not to have come, as there is no one besides yourself to look after your house."

"Not come," said the old man as angrily as before; "three periods of my life [1] have passed, and one only remains; if I am not to look after my soul now, then when shall I?"

The young man said—

"If I rightly understand the Shasters,[2] one can save one's soul just as well by remaining at home as by visiting places of pilgrimage."

[1] It is considered that life consists of four stages, viz., *Brahmachorjya*, *Garhasthya*, *Bánprosthya*, and *Bhoikhya*. The first consists of studying and practising the precepts of the Vedas; the second of marital life and the performance of domestic duties; the third stage is abandonment of the world and leading the life of a hermit in the jungles; the fourth and last is the stage of religious mendicancy.

[2] The word "Shasters" means books written by the gods or celebrated Munees (Sages), the mythology of the Hindus, comprising the Beds, Tantras, Puráns, &c.

"Then why did you come?" asked the old man.

The young man replied—

"I told you before that I wished very much to see the ocean, and it is simply on that account that I have come." Then, in a lower tone, he muttered, "Ah! what have I seen! I shall never forget it even in subsequent states of existence!"[1]

The old man took no heed of the poetry, but was intently listening to the conversation of the sailors. One of them was saying to another, "O brother, so big a business has ended badly; I cannot understand what outer ocean we have fallen into, or what country we have come to."

The speaker's voice evinced considerable fear, and the old man gathered that some danger had arisen to cause anxiety.

"What's the matter, boatman?" he asked

[1] This passage refers to the doctrine of metempsychosis or transmigration of souls. A devoted wife often says to her husband, "What virtuous acts (*punya*) I must have done in a former birth to get a husband like you!" or, "In a future life may I have a husband like you!"

with quaking heart, but the boatman gave no reply. However, the young man didn't wait for a reply, but, coming out on deck, saw that it was almost dawn, and that a very dense fog had enveloped everything. Sky, stars, moon, or bank, nothing whatever could be seen in any direction. He saw that the boatmen had lost their way, and that now there was no certainty as to what direction they were going in. He was terrified lest they should go out to sea and be wrecked in the open.

The passengers could not see anything of all this from inside the boat, owing to an awning which was placed in front to keep out the cold; but the young pilgrim took in the whole situation, and explained it to the old man. Then there arose a great uproar in the boat; some of the women inside had been awakened by the noise, and, hearing what was the matter, raised cries of distress. The old man said, "Get to the bank, get to the bank."

The young man said with a smile, "Our case wouldn't be so bad, if we only knew where the bank was." Hearing this, the travellers redoubled their cries. The young man with difficulty succeeded in calming them, and said to the sailors, "There is no cause whatever for anxiety; it is now dawn, and the sun is sure to rise within a few *dandas*;[1] the boat cannot possibly be wrecked within so short a time. Stop rowing for the present, and let the boat go wherever the current takes her. Afterwards, when the sun comes out, we will consider what to do."

The boatmen agreed to this course, and acted accordingly. For a long time they remained idle, while the pilgrims' hearts were in their mouths from fear. As there was not a breath of wind, they could not feel the movement of the waves; nevertheless, they all regarded death as certain. The men began noiselessly to repeat[2] the name of Durga,[3] while

[1] According to Bengali time, the day and night are divided into eight *prahars* of four hours each. The prahar is subdivided into *dandas*.

[2] The Bengali word is "*jap*." It means to repeat a religious formula over and over again.

[3] Durga, the wife of Shib or Mahadeb, otherwise known as Káli, Bhoirobi, &c.

the women cried and shrieked in various ways. One of the women had abandoned her child at Gangá-ságor; she had flung it into the water, and had not been able to recover it. She only did not weep.

While they were thus waiting, it got to about one *pahar* of the day, when suddenly the boatmen made a great noise by calling out the names of the five Pirs[1] of the ocean. The pilgrims all asked, "What is it, manjhi?[2] what has happened?" The boatmen with one voice roared out, "The sun is coming out, the sun is coming out; land, land, land!" The pilgrims eagerly came outside on deck, and began to inspect the situation. They saw that the sun had come out, and on all

[1] A Pir is a Mohammedan saint. The Mohammedans are *par excellence* the sailors and boatmen of Bengal. The two great classes of the population, Hindoos and Mohammedans, often show a mutual respect for one another's gods and religious festivals. I have seen Mussulmans fired by a sort of religious enthusiasm both during the Durga pooja and at the pulling of a Juggernath car (Ruth Jattra). I have also seen Hindus make a sort of obeisance on passing a Mussulman mosque, and when the Mohurrum is going on the lower castes of Hindus have *taboots* and *tazeahs* made, and carry them along with the Mussulmans.

[2] Manjhi = a boatman or rower.

sides the darkness and mist had cleared away. About one *pahar* of the day had passed. The place they had come to was not actually the outer ocean, but merely the mouth of the river; still, the river at that point was wider than anywhere else. Though one bank of the river was quite close to the boat—not more than five hundred cubits away—no trace of the other bank could be seen. In whatever direction one looked, an endless mass of water, sparkling in the flickering rays of the sun, mingled with the sky on the utmost horizon. Close by, the water was very muddy, like the colour of river water, but in the distance it was bright blue. The passengers concluded for certain that they had been carried into the outer ocean; still, it was fortunate the bank was close, and there was therefore no cause for anxiety. They ascertained their position from the sun, and had no difficulty in perceiving that the bank in front of them was the western bank of the ocean. In the centre of the bank, not far from the boat, a stream was slowly falling into the ocean like a streak of gold. At the point of junction on the right bank countless birds were sporting on an enormous heap of sand. This river is now known as "the Rasulpur river."

CHAPTER II.

ON THE BANK.

THE excitement of the passengers having subsided, the boatmen remarked that the tide would not set in just yet, and proposed that they should pass the interval in cooking their food on the bank, and afterwards, when the tide commenced to rise, they might start for their own country. The passengers having assented to this proposition, the boatmen fastened the boat to the bank. The pilgrims then got out and busied themselves with their bathing and other matutinal rites. Having finished these, a fresh obstacle in the way of cooking presented itself. There was no firewood in the boat, and for fear of tigers no one was willing to collect any from the land above. At last, seeing that everybody was likely to starve, the old man said to the young man whom we have mentioned above—

"My dear Nobokumar, if you don't devise some remedy for this, the whole lot of us will die."

Nobokumar pondered for a moment and said—

"Very well, I will go. Give me an axe, and let somebody accompany me with a bill-hook." No one wished to go with Nobokumar. "We shall see about it at dinner time," said Nobokumar, and girding up his loins, he went alone, axe in hand, to bring the wood.

Ascending the bank Nobokumar saw that as far as the eye could reach there was no trace of human habitation anywhere, but only jungle. The jungle, however, was not a dense forest, nor did it consist of big trees; simply patches of ground here and there were covered with small bushes, in which Nobokumar saw no wood worth cutting. So he had to go further from the river-bank in search of a suitable tree. At last he found one worth cutting, and took from it as much wood as he required.

To carry away the wood now appeared to be an insurmountable difficulty. Nobokumar, not being a poor man's son, was not accustomed to such labour. He had come in quest of wood without considering all the difficulties, and now the conveyance of the wood was by no means an easy matter. Still he had commenced the task, and Nobokumar was not a man to be deterred by a trifle. So somehow or other he began to bring away the wood, and came along with it, alternately carrying it and sitting down to rest a little.

Nobokumar's return was thus delayed, and here his comrades began to get anxious. They feared that he had been eaten up by tigers, and when the probable time for his return had passed, their fear became certainty. Still not one of them had the courage to ascend the bank and go a short distance in quest of him.

While the pilgrims were thus cogitating, a terrible noise arose in the midst of the waters. The boatmen saw that the tide was rising, and they were well aware that, when the tide rises in these parts, the waves dash with such violence against the bank, that boats remaining near it are broken to pieces. For this reason, they in great haste loosed the boat's moorings, and pushed into mid-stream; almost before they had done so, the sand was covered with water, and the pilgrims only just had time to jump hurriedly into the boat. The rice and other provisions on the *chur*[1] were all washed away. Unfortunately, the boatmen were not very skilful, and could not control the boat, which was swiftly carried by the strength of the current up the Rasulpur river. One of the passengers remarked that Nobokumar had been left behind. "What!" quoth another, "d'you suppose your Nobokumar's alive? Jackals have eaten him up."

The force of the current was taking the boat up the Rasulpur river, and the boatmen, knowing how hard it would be to return,

[1] *Chur* is an island in the middle of a river. Such islands are frequently thrown up during a rainy season in the large rivers of Bengal. They belong to Government, provided the passage between them and the mainland be not fordable.

were striving with all their might and main to bring her out. So violent were their efforts, that even in that month of Mágh drops of sweat stood out on their foreheads. Though they succeeded in bringing her out of the Rasulpur river, still, no sooner had she come out than the force of the current at that spot drove her northwards with the speed of an arrow. The boatmen could not stop her for a moment, and the boat returned no more.

When the current had subsided to such an extent as to admit of the movements of the boat being controlled, they had come a long distance from the mouth of the Rasulpur river. It now became necessary to decide whether they should return or not for Nobokumar, and here we should mention that Nobokumar's fellow-pilgrims were merely his neighbours, and neither his relatives nor kinsmen. They took into consideration the fact that to return from there meant waiting for the next ebb-tide; night would arrive, when they could not proceed, and they would therefore have to wait for the next day's tide; till then, all would have to remain without food, and they would be almost dead after two days' fasting. Moreover, the boatmen were unwilling to return, and were not amenable to orders. As they alleged, it was probable Nobokumar had been killed by tigers, and therefore what was the good of taking so much trouble?

With such reflections the pilgrims came to the conclusion that it was best to return without Nobokumar, who was thus left to his fate in that terrible forest by the sea.

If any one, on hearing this, should resolve never to go in quest of wood to assuage a neighbour's hunger, he is vile, vile as these pilgrims were. Those who are of such a nature that they can once abandon a benefactor in the desert, will always do so; while, no matter how often he may be abandoned, the man, whose nature it is to do so, will again and again go and collect wood for another. Your being a villain is no reason why I should not show my own worth.

CHAPTER III.

SOLITUDE.

AT the present time two small villages, Dowlutpur and Daryápur, stand near the spot where Nobokumar was abandoned by his companions; but at the time of our story there was no trace of human habitation in those parts—it was nothing but forest. Still the country was not so uniformly level as other parts of Bengal. For several leagues without interruption, from the Rasulpur mouth as far as the river Suborna-rekha, the country was studded with numerous sand-heaps, which, had they been a little higher, might have deserved the name of small hills; at the present time they are known as "Báliári." The white summits of these sand-hills look very beautiful from a distance in the rays of the mid-day sun. There are no big trees on the top; below there is a growth of small jungle, while the centre and summits are conspicuous by the brilliance of an almost spotless white. Small bushes, wild shrubs, and flowers abound midst the vegetation that encircles the base of these hillocks.

Such was the inhospitable region in which Nobokumar was abandoned by his comrades. First of all, on coming to the river-bank with his load of wood, he could not see the boat. Though this caused him a sudden pang of fear, he could not believe that his comrades had altogether abandoned him. He supposed that, on the sand being covered by the rising tide, they had moored the boat on some other place hard by, and would quickly return to look for him. In this expectation, he sate there for some time and waited, but no boat came. Nor could he see any of the pilgrims. Nobokumar became very faint with hunger, and not being able to wait any longer, he went along the river-bank looking for the boat. He saw no trace of it anywhere, and returned to the same spot. He thought that the force of the tide must have floated it away, and that his comrades were delayed in returning by the hostile current. But the tide came to an end, and then he thought that the boat could not return against the tide owing to the force of the hostile current, but that it must be now returning with the ebb-tide. But the ebb-tide, too, gradually increased—gradually it got later and later, till the sun set! If the boat had been returning, it must have returned ere now.

Then Nobokumar felt certain that either the boat had been swamped by the tidal waves, or that his companions had abandoned him; and with the uprising of this certainty Nobokumar's heart was crushed within him, just as a man walking under a hill is crushed by a piece of the summit falling upon him.

At this juncture Nobokumar's state of mind was beyond description. Though he was pained with doubt concerning the possible destruction of his comrades, still he speedily forgot such sorrow in the contemplation of his own danger, especially as grief gave place to anger when it occurred to him that his comrades might have abandoned him.

Nobokumar saw that there was no village near, no shelter, no people, nothing to eat and nothing to drink; the river-water was unbearably salt, and he was beginning to suffer agonies from hunger and thirst. There was no shelter, nor even had he any covering to keep out the bitter cold; he would have to sleep without roof and without covering under the frosty sky on the bank of that river, tossed by the wind, made cold with dew. It might be that tigers or bears would kill him during the night, or if not to-night, at any rate to-morrow; death was a certainty.

Excitement prevented Nobokumar from sitting long in one place. Leaving the bank, he ascended the higher land, and began to wander hither and thither. Gradually it got dark; in the cold sky the stars began silently to burst forth, just as they burst forth in Nobokumar's own country. In the darkness everywhere was solitude; sky, forest, sea, all was still, save for the ceaseless rolling of the ocean and the fitful roar of some wild beast. Nevertheless, in that darkness, and under that chilly sky, Nobokumar kept wandering midst the sand-hills, now in the valley, then on the table-land, now beneath the sand-hills, and then on their summits. Each step he walked there was a probability of his being attacked by wild animals; but there was none the less cause for fear even if he remained sitting in one place.

Nobokumar became weary with wandering about, and the fact that he had had no food all day made him the more exhausted. He rested his back against a sand-heap and sate down, and thought of his warm bed at home. When the weariness of bodily or mental toil brings on melancholy, then sleep almost invariably comes along with it. Nobokumar fell asleep in the midst of his pondering. If such were not the rule of nature, we could not always bear up against the terrible shock of worldly troubles.

CHAPTER IV.

ON THE SUMMIT OF THE SAND-HILL.

WHEN Nobokumar awoke it was the depth of night. He thought it a wonder that he had not already been killed by tigers, and began to peer about to see if any tigers were coming. Suddenly he saw a light in front at a great distance. Lest he might be the victim of a delusion, Nobokumar began to watch the light attentively. Its circumference gradually increased and became brighter; he felt certain that it was the light of a fire, and with this certainty his hopes of life revived. Such a light could only issue from the habitation of man. Nobokumar got up, and ran in the direction of the light. At one time he thought, "Is this some ghostly light? It may be, still there can be no safety for the man who desists from mere fear." Thinking this, he went forward fearlessly, keeping the light in view. At every step trees, creepers, and sand-hillocks obstructed his path; still he pressed on, trampling down the creepers and leaping over the sand-hillocks. On getting near the light, he saw that a fire was burning on the summit of a very lofty sand-hill, and in its glare a human form, seated on the top, stood out like a picture against the canvas of the sky. Nobokumar determined to approach the man, and pressed forward with firm footsteps. At last he began to ascend the hill. Then he began to be a little afraid; still, with untrembling footsteps, he continued to ascend the hill. Coming in front of the seated form, his hair stood on end with what he saw. He was uncertain whether to remain or to go back.

The form seated on the summit was meditating[1] with closed eyes, and did not at first

[1] The Bengali word is "*dhyán,*" which literally means contemplation of the immortal Brahma. The generic word for religious meditation is "*jóg.*"

observe Nobokumar. The latter saw that his age was about fifty, but could not perceive whether he had on any cotton clothing. A tiger-skin covered him from his waist to his knees; a necklace of *rudrak* seeds was on his throat, and the broad circle of his face was surrounded with matted hair and beard. In front of him a wood-fire was burning: it was by the light of this fire that Nobokumar had been able to find his way there. Nobokumar perceived a terrible smell, and on looking at his seat was able to ascertain the cause. The form with matted hair was seated on a headless, putrid corpse. His fear increased when he saw on the ground in front a human skull containing some red liquid substance. The ground on all sides was strewed with bones—there were even small pieces of bone in the seed necklace on the devotee's throat. Nobokumar stood like one stupefied with incantations. He could not make up his mind whether to advance or to flee. He had heard of Kapáliks, and knew that this being must be a terrible Kapálik.[1]

At the time of Nobokumar's arrival, the Kapálik was absorbed in incantations, or *jup*, or contemplation. Seeing Nobokumar, he did not even raise his eyebrows. After a long time he asked, "Who are you?" Nobokumar replied, "A Brahman."

The Kapálik said "Stay," and resumed his former occupation. Nobokumar stood and waited.

[1] Kapáliks are supposed to have existed until quite recently. They worshipped Siva and his terrible consort by means of human sacrifices. The sacrifice of goats, which now goes on at Kalighát (whence the name of Calcutta), is but the more civilised outcome of the old sacrifices.

The Tantras represent a phase of Hinduism generally later than that of the Puranas. The principal Hindu deities are sometimes supposed to possess a double nature—one quiescent, the other active. The active energising will (Sakti) of a god is personified as his wife, or sometimes as the female half of his essence. The white or mild nature of Siva includes the Saktis Uma, Gauri, Lukshmi, Saraswati, &c.; the black or fierce nature includes Durga, Kali, Kamuna, Kandi, Bhoirobi, &c. As destruction was more dreaded than creation or preservation, so the wife of the god Siva, presiding over dissolution, and called Kali, Durga, Devi, Parbotti, &c., became the most important personage in the whole Pantheon to that great majority of worshippers whose religion was actuated by superstitious fears.

In this way half a *pahar* passed away. At last the Kapálik got up and said to Nobokumar in Sanskrit, as before, "Follow me."

It is certain that Nobokumar would never have consented to do so at any other time, but now he was dying of hunger and thirst, and he therefore replied, "As my master wishes; but I am suffering terribly from hunger and thirst; please inform me where I can get something to eat."

The Kapálik said, "You have been sent by Bhoirobi; come with me, and you will get food."

Nobokumar followed the Kapálik. On the road neither uttered a word, though they travelled a long distance. At last they got to a leaf-hut. The Kapálik entered first, and told Nobokumar to enter. By some means which Nobokumar could not understand, he struck a light with a piece of wood, which enabled Nobokumar to perceive that the hut was entirely made of the leaves of the *kia* tree. Inside were several tiger skins, a pot of water, some fruits and roots.

The Kapálik lighted a fire, and said, "You may eat all the fruits and roots: make a vessel from the leaves, and drink from the pot of water. There is a tiger skin; if you want to sleep, do so: be at your ease, and don't fear the tigers. After you have slept, I will talk with you. Don't leave the hut till you have seen me." With these words the Kapálik went away. Nobokumar devoured the few fruits and roots that were there, drank the somewhat bitter water, and was thereby much refreshed. Then he lay down on the tiger skin, and, thanks to his hard day's work, speedily fell asleep.

CHAPTER V.

ON THE BRINK OF THE OCEAN.

On getting up at dawn, Nobokumar naturally felt anxious to devise some means for getting home, especially as the proximity of this Kapálik did not at all please him. But for the present how was he to get out of this pathless jungle? Again, how was he to know the way home? The Kapálik must know the way: surely he would tell it if asked, especially as so far he had done nothing to cause him alarm. Then why should he be afraid? The Kapálik had forbidden him to leave the hut before his return, and he would incur his anger by disobedience. Nobokumar had heard that Kapáliks can, by the strength of their incantations, accomplish the impossible—therefore he ought not to disobey him.

Thinking this, and much besides, Nobokumar made up his mind to remain in the hut for the present.

Gradually it became afternoon, but the Kapálik did not return. Yesterday's fast, and the fact that he had eaten nothing to-day, made his hunger intense. He had consumed the previous night the few roots and herbs that were in the hut, and now, if he were not to go in search of some more he would die of hunger. When a little of the day was left, Nobokumar was driven by the pangs of hunger to leave the hut in quest of food.

Nobokumar wandered in and out the adjacent sand-hills in search of roots. He tasted the fruit of several trees growing on the sand, and found that the fruit of one of the trees was very sweet, like almonds, and thereby satisfied his hunger.

The above-mentioned sand-heaps were very narrow, so that Nobokumar easily wandered beyond them. Then he came upon a sandless dense forest. Those who have wandered for a short time in an unknown forest, know that one can lose one's way in a moment. This was just what happened to Nobokumar. After he had come a little way, he could not make out by what path he had left the hermitage. A deep noise of water fell upon his ear, and he knew that this must be the rumbling of the ocean. After a moment he suddenly emerged from the forest, and saw the sea in front of him. The sight of that immense, endless mass of blue water made his heart overflow with intense joy. He went and sate down on the sandy shore. The foaming blue, the endless sea! On both sides, as far as the eye could reach, could be seen the streaks of foam flung by the breaking of the waves, like garlands woven with heaps of pure white flowers. Those white streaks on the golden sand formed a fitting hair-ornament for the jungle-belted earth. In the midst of the blue ocean, too, the foamy waves were breaking in a thousand places. If so strong a wind could blow as to move the stars from their myriad resting-places, and dash them about in the azure sky, they would resemble the gambols of those ocean-waves. At this moment a portion of the blue water was burning like molten gold in the soft rays of the setting sun. In the far distance the vessel of some European trader was sailing on the heart of the ocean, spreading its wings like some large bird.

As long as Nobokumar was seated on the shore, gazing intently at the beauty of the ocean, he was deprived of the sense of space. Then all at once twilight descended and sat on the black waters. Then Nobokumar remembered that he must look for the hermitage. Heaving a deep sigh he got up. Why he heaved a deep sigh is more than I can say. Perhaps it was the recollection of some past happiness, who can tell? He got up and returned towards the sea, and as he turned an incomparable sight met his gaze. There, on the sandy shore, on the brink of the deep-sounding ocean, in the dim twilight, stood a wondrous female form! Masses of hair, unconfined, curling like snakes, falling in a heap to the ankles. Against the hair stood out a jewel form, like a painting on the painter's canvas. The abundance of her curly tresses prevented the whole of her face from being seen; nevertheless it could be seen like the moon's rays bursting forth from a cleft in the clouds. The glance from her large eyes was very steady, very sweet, intensely deep, and full of light. That glance was tender and bright like the moon's rays playing on the heart of the sea. Her heaps of hair had covered her shoulders and arms; the former were quite invisible, but the marble brilliancy of her arms could be seen a little. The girl's body was entirely devoid of ornaments. There was a certain charm in her form that it is impossible to describe. Her colour was like the lustre of the half-moon, her hair jet black. The beauty of the skin and hair was enhanced by their close contiguity. One could only feel its wondrous power of fascination by seeing it in the evening light, on the shore of that deep-resounding ocean!

Nobokumar stood motionless on the apparition of this heavenly form in so inaccessible a forest. He was deprived of the power of speech, and gazed in silent wonderment. The woman, too, was motionless, and with a steady gaze fixed her large eyes on Nobokumar's face. The difference between them was this, that Nobokumar's glance was that of a startled being, while the woman's look bore no trace of astonishment, though it evinced considerable anxiety.

Thus, on the lonely shore of the ocean, they gazed at one another for some time. After a long interval, the woman's voice was heard. She said very softly—

"Traveller, have you lost your way?"

The harp of Nobokumar's heart sounded in unison with this voice. Sometimes the strings of the wondrous heart's mechanism are so devoid of tune, that, try as hard as we may, we cannot unite them. But they are corrected by a single sound, naught but the voice of a woman. Then all becomes tuneful. From that moment life appears as happy as a current of music. So that voice sounded in Nobokumar's ear.

"Traveller, have you lost your way?" This was the sound that penetrated Nobokumar's ear. What was the meaning, what reply to give, he could not think. The sound appeared to wander about, as if quivering with joy; it appeared to flow on the wind; it was murmured by the leaves of the trees, and then seemed to grow fainter and melt away in the noise of the sea. The ocean-girt earth was beautiful; the woman was beautiful; the voice, too, was beautiful. The tune of beauty rose on the strings of his heart.

The woman, getting no reply, said, "Come." So saying, she went away: her steps could not be seen. Softly, and with invisible tread, she went, like a white cloud moved by the gentle wind in spring-time. Nobokumar went with her like a mechanical doll. In one place they would have to go round a small patch of jungle. On getting behind this, he could not observe the woman any more; when he had got round it, he saw the hut in front of him.

CHAPTER VI.

WITH THE KAPÁLIK.

NOBOKUMAR entered the hut, and, closing the door, buried his head in his hands. He did not quickly raise his head again.

"Is this a goddess, a human being, or merely the Kapálik's magic?" Nobokumar breathlessly commenced to revolve this matter in his mind, but could make nothing of it.

Owing to his reverie, Nobokumar had not noticed another wonder. Before his arrival a piece of wood was burning in the hut. Then afterwards, late at night, when he remembered that he had not performed his evening rites—then, giving up all anxiety on account of water, he understood the extraordinary aspect of the affair. There was not only a light, but rice and other things ready for cooking. Nobokumar was not astonished—he thought that this, too, must be the Kapálik's work—in such a place there was no cause for astonishment. After performing his evening rites he cooked the rice and other eatables in an earthen vessel he had found in the hut and satisfied his hunger.

The next morning he rose from his bed of skins, and went towards the sea-shore. Thanks to his wanderings of the day before, he knew his way to-day without much difficulty. There he performed his morning rites and waited. For whom was he waiting? How strong Nobokumar's hope was that the enchantress he had before seen would again come there, I cannot say, but he could not leave that place. He waited long, but no one came there. Then Nobokumar began to wander in every direction, keeping close to that place, but his search was fruitless. He could not even perceive a trace of the presence of any human being. He again returned and sate down in the same place. The sun set, and darkness came on. In despair Nobokumar returned to the hut. Returning from the sea-shore at evening Nobokumar saw that the Kapálik was seated in silence on the ground inside the hut. Nobokumar at once wished him good evening, but the Kapálik made no reply.

Nobokumar said, "Why have I been deprived up till now of the pleasure of seeing my lord?" The Kapálik said, "I was engaged in the performance of a peculiar vow."

Nobokumar spoke of his desire to go home, and said, "I don't know the way, and have no expenses. I was in hopes of seeing my master and obtaining suitable instructions from him."

The Kapálik simply said, "Come with me." And with this word the ascetic got up. Nobokumar followed him in the hopes of finding some means of getting home.

The light of evening had not yet faded away. The Kapálik went in front, and Nobokumar behind. Suddenly Nobokumar felt a soft touch on his back, and turning round, he was transfixed by what he saw—that sylvan goddess form, with thick and luxuriant tresses hanging to her ankles! noiseless and motionless as before! Whence had that sudden apparition come behind him? Nobokumar saw that the woman had her finger on her lips, and understood that she was forbidding him to speak. Nor was there much necessity for such prohibition, for what was Nobokumar to say? There he stood, filled with astonishment. The Kapálik went on in front, and saw nothing of all this. When they were out of his hearing, the woman said something in a soft voice, and these were the sounds that entered Nobokumar's ear—

"Where are you going? Do not go—return—flee!"

Having said this, the speaker disappeared without waiting for a reply. For some moments Nobokumar stood dumfoundered. He was eager to follow the woman, but he could not make out in what direction she had gone. He thought, "Whose magic is this? or am I under a delusion? These words indicate danger, but danger of what? Tantriks can accomplish everything—then why should I flee? Where am I to flee to?"

Nobokumar was thus pondering, when he saw that the Kapálik had missed him and was returning. The Kapálik said, "Why are you delaying?" When a man is in doubt what to do, he goes wherever he happens to be first called. On the Kapálik calling a second time, Nobokumar followed him without a word.

Going some distance he saw a hut with a dead wall (you might call it a hut or a small house, but we need not concern ourselves with that). Behind it was the sandy beach of the sea. The Kapálik was taking Nobokumar past the hut to the shore, when like an arrow the woman he had seen before swiftly passed by his side, and whispered in his ear as she passed—"Flee, even now—don't you know that the Tantrik's worship consists of human flesh?"

The sweat came out on Nobokumar's brow. Unfortunately the Kapálik overheard these words, and said—"Kopal-Kundala!"

To Nobokumar the voice sounded like

thunder, but Kopal-Kundala made no reply.

The Kapálik seized Nobokumar's hand and began to drag him along. At the murderer's touch Nobokumar's blood coursed through his veins with a hundred-fold more violence. His lost courage returned, and he said—"Release my hand."

The Kapálik made no reply. Again Nobokumar asked, "Where are you taking me to?"

The Kapálik said, "To the place of sacrifice." "Why?" said Nobokumar. "To slay you," replied the Kapálik.

Nobokumar pulled away his hand with all the strength he could muster, and such was the force he used, that any ordinary person would have been felled to the earth, much less could have held him. But the Kapálik did not even move a muscle. Nobokumar's wrist remained in his grasp, and he felt as if his bones were broken. Nobokumar followed the Kapálik like one on the point of death.

On coming to the sand Nobokumar saw that a large wood fire was burning as on the day before. Round about were strewn the things required for a Tantrik's *pooja*, and among them a human skull full of wine; but there was no corpse. Nobokumar inferred that he was to be the corpse.

Some dry and tough stalks of creepers were already collected there, and the Kapálik commenced to bind Nobokumar firmly. Nobokumar struggled with all his might, but his struggles were of no avail whatever. He found that, old as he was, the Kapálik had the strength of a mad elephant. Seeing Nobokumar's struggles, the Kapálik said, "Fool, why do you struggle? your birth is to-day fruitful; this ball of flesh of yours will be devoted to the worship of Durga; what greater piece of luck can befall a man like you?"

The Kapálik tied Nobokumar firmly, and flung him on the sand; and then commenced to perform the rites preliminary to sacrifice.

The dry creeper-stalks were very tough—

the fetters were very firm—death was near! Nobokumar consigned his soul to the mercy of his tutelary god. First he thought of his native land, and his happy home; then, as the faces of his father and mother far away came into his recollection, he shed one or two tears, which were sucked in by the sand. When the Kapálik had finished the rites preliminary to sacrifice, he left his seat to get a good sword. But, strange to say, he could not find it where he had left it. He was a little astonished, as he well remembered having put it in its proper place that afternoon. He had not removed it since; then where had it gone? The Kapálik looked for it here and there, but could not find it. Then he went towards the hut above-mentioned, and called Kopal-Kundala. But, though he called again and again, Kopal-Kundala gave no answer. Then the Kapálik's eyes became red, and his eyebrows were knitted. As he ran towards the house, Nobokumar seized the opportunity and tried once more to burst his fetters asunder, but his efforts were of no avail.

At this moment there was a tender footstep close by on the sand; it was not the Kapálik's footstep. Nobokumar looked round and saw that enchantress—Kopal-Kundala! A sword was swinging in her hand.

Kopal-Kundala said, "Quiet, do not speak. The sword is with me; I have stolen it."

So saying Kopal-Kundala quickly began to cut Nobokumar's fetters with the sword, and in a moment released him. "Flee," she said; "follow me, I will show the way."

So saying, Kopal-Kundala went like an arrow showing the way. Nobokumar leapt along behind her.

CHAPTER VII.

THE SEARCH.

In this direction the Kapálik searched every nook and corner of the house, and seeing neither the sword nor Kopal-Kundala, he felt suspicious, and returned to the sea-shore. On arriving there, he saw that Nobokumar had disappeared. At this he was dumfoundered. After a few moments his gaze fell on the torn stalk-fetters. Then, realising the truth, the Kapálik ran in search of Nobokumar. But it was impossible to know in what direction or by what path the fugitives had gone in that solitary forest. The darkness prevented him from seeing any one, and so he wandered about for a moment or two, trying to catch the sound of voices, but he could not regularly hear them. For this reason he ascended to the summit of a high sand-heap, in order to get a good view all round. On the other side from that by which the Kapálik ascended, the base of the hill had been washed away by the storm-water. The Kapálik did not know this, and immediately the weight of his body pressed on it, the summit broke and fell with a terrible crash; and as it fell, the Kapálik fell along with it, like a buffalo hurled from some mountain-peak.

CHAPTER VIII.

IN THE HERMITAGE.

In that pitch dark amabosia[1] night the two fugitives hastily entered the forest. Nobokumar did not know the jungle paths, and all he could do was to follow the lead of his fair companion of sixteen. But, owing to the forest and the darkness, he lost sight of her now and again, as the young girl ran in one direction and he in another. The girl told him to catch hold of her skirt, which Nobokumar did. They gradually came along with soft footsteps. Nothing was visible in the darkness, except that now and again the white summit of some sand-hill was dimly seen in

[1] The month is divided into two halves, the light half and the dark half of the moon. The amabosia is the last day of the dark half, that is, the darkest night of the month.

the light of stars; and here and there the limbs of some tree covered with fire-flies.

Kopal-Kundala came with our traveller to a secret forest. It was then midnight. In front could be seen in the darkness the dome of a very lofty temple, and near it a house encompassed with a brick wall. Kopal-Kundala approached a door in the wall and knocked at it. After she had knocked several times, a voice from within said, "Who is it? Kopal-Kundala, I suppose?"

Kopal-Kundala said, "Open the door."

The speaker opened the door. He was the Sebok[1] or Adhikari of the goddess to whom the temple was consecrated. His age was over fifty. Kopal-Kundala took his head of scanty locks in her hands, drew his ear near her mouth, and in a few words explained the situation of her companion. The Adhikari buried his head in his hand and began to ponder. At last he said, "This is a very

[1] Sebok, he who does *seba* or worship, a priest. The word *seba* also means any service. A wife is said to serve her husband well. A sweeper speaks of his occupation as "*gañer seba*" (service for the village).

difficult matter. The great man can accomplish whatever he wishes. However that may be, by the favour of the mother[1] no harm will befall you. Where is the man?"

Kopal-Kundala beckoned Nobokumar to approach. Nobokumar, who had been standing in a corner outside, entered the house. The Adhikari said to him, "Conceal yourself here for to-day; to-morrow morning I will show you the road to Midnapur."

In the course of conversation the Adhikari came to know that Nobokumar had not yet eaten anything. He commenced to make preparations for his food, but Nobokumar was very loth to eat, and only asked for a resting-place. The Adhikari prepared a bed for Nobokumar in his own cook-house, and when the latter had gone to lie down, Kopal-Kundala got herself ready to return to the sea-shore. The Adhikari looked at her affectionately, and

[1] The mother, *i.e.* Kali or Durga. Goddesses are frequently spoken of and addressed as mother; as, for instance, the Ganges, "Gangá má."

said, "Don't go; wait a moment. I have a favour to ask you."

Kopal-Kundala. What is it?

Adhikari. I have called you mother[1] ever since I have known you. I can touch the feet of the goddess and swear that I love you more than a mother. You must not refuse my request.

Kopa. I won't.

Adhi. My request is this, that you should not return there.

Kopa. Why?

Adhi. If you do, you will certainly be killed.

Kopa. I know that.

Adhi. Then why do you ask me?

Kopa. If I don't go there, where am I to go to?

Adhi. Go with this traveller to another country.

[1] Parents frequently address their children affectionately as mother and father. In Orissa old women sometimes address young girls with whom they are on familiar terms as "*mousi*" (aunt); and Brahman children call their mothers "*Bo*" or "*Bohu*," which means daughter-in-law, or the young girl of the family.

Kopal-Kundala remained silent. The Adhikari said, "Mother, what are you thinking about?"

Kopa. When your disciple came here, then you said that it was not right for a young woman to go with a young man. Why, then, do you tell me to do so now?

Adhi. Then I had no fears for your life, nor had I any good plan for your escape. Now a good opportunity offers. Come, let us take the permission of the mother.

So saying, the Adhikari, light in hand, went to the entrance of the temple and opened the door; Kopal-Kundala, too, went with him. In the temple was a life-size statue of the destroyer Kali, to which both of them reverently bowed down. The Adhikari washed his body, and plucked an entire bael-leaf from a vessel of flowers, and having sanctified it with *mantras*, he placed it at the feet of the image, and looked at it. Then, after a moment, he said to Kopal-Kundala, "Look, mother; the goddess has accepted the offering. The bael-leaf has not fallen; the purpose for which I gave the offering will of a surety turn out well. You may go without fear with this traveller. But I am well aware of the character and customs of people of the world. If you go in close companionship with this man, he will be put to shame in society for taking an unknown young woman with him. You, too, will be looked down upon. You have told me that he is a Brahman youth, and I have seen the sacrificial thread on his neck. If he marries you, and takes you, then all will be proper; otherwise, I too could not advise you to go with him."

"Marries me!" Kopal-Kundala uttered this word very softly, and said, "I have heard the word marriage from your mouth, but I don't exactly know what it is. What shall I have to do?"

The Adhikari said with a smile, "For women marriage is the only stepping-stone to religion. For this reason a wife is called *Shaha-dharmini.*[1] Even the mother of the world is the wife of Siva."

[1] *Shaha-dharmini.* Literally, she who worships along with her husband. Now-a-days the wife may almost be called the

The Adhikari thought he had explained everything, and Kopal-Kundala thought she understood everything. She said, "Let it be so, but I do not feel inclined to abandon him who has supported me for so long."

Adhi. Don't you know why he has supported you? Don't you know that the Tantrik's mission is only accomplished by destroying the chastity of a woman? I too have studied the Tantras. Mother Juggadumba is the mother of the earth. She is the quintessence of chastity—the queen of chaste women—she never accepts worship that consists of destroying chastity. It is for this reason that I am thwarting the desire of the great man. If you flee, he will never be ungrateful! It is only because the proper

husband's substitute in matters of worship. On religious holidays the men of the educated class do not do *pooja*, but leave their womenkind to do it, just as in England the wife often goes to church for herself and husband also. Women of the upper and middle classes make pilgrimages to Gya and Kási (Benares) and offer up the *pindas* (sacrificial cakes) for their own as well as for their husband's ancestors, and such *pooja* is supposed to be as, or nearly as, efficacious as if performed by their husbands.

moment has not yet arrived that you have hitherto escaped destruction. Considering what you have done to-day, there is fear for your life. Therefore I tell you to flee. This, too, is Bhobani's order. So go; if I had the means of keeping you back, I would do so, but you know I cannot.

Kopa. Let it be marriage then.

After this conversation they both came out of the temple. The Adhikari seated Kopal-Kundala in one room, and then, going to Nobokumar's bed, he sate down by his pillow and said, "Are you asleep, sir?"

Nobokumar was not in the mood for sleep. He was thinking of his lot, and replied, "No, sir."

The Adhikari said, "I have come to ask you who you are. Are you a Brahman?"

Nob. "Yes." "What class?" "Rarhi."

Adhi. We also are Rarhi Brahmans; do not suppose I am an Orissa Brahman. Our family are astrologers, though I am now a servant of the mother. What is your name?

Nob. "Nobokumar Sarma." "Your country ?" "Septogram." "What village ?" "Bonyagháti." "How many wives have you ?" "One only."

Nobokumar did not reveal everything, for, as a matter of fact, he had not even one wife. He had married Podmaboti, the daughter of Ramgobind Ghosal. After the marriage Podmaboti remained for some time in her father's house, and now and then used to visit her father-in-law's house. When she was thirteen years of age, her father had taken his whole family to Purustom [1] on pilgrimage. At that time the Pathans, driven out of Bengal by Akber Shah, were living with their followers in Orissa. Akber set on foot a regular attempt to subjugate them; and at the time Ramgobind Ghosal was returning from Orissa, the war be-

[1] Purustom or Puri, where is the Temple of Jagannáth. Hither resort from all parts of India except the extreme south the worshippers of Vishnu. The temple and worship were originally Buddhist, as is evident from several peculiarities that still exist. For instance, the sweetmeal or "*mahápras'ád*" sold at the temple may be carried away by a man of low caste, and then eaten even by a Brahman. I believe the fact of its passing through the hands of a Mussulman would not prevent the holiest of Hindoos from eating it.

tween the Moguls and Pathans had commenced. As he was on his return journey, he fell into the hands of the Pathans, who at that time were quite uncivilised. For the sake of money, they maltreated the innocent traveller. Ramgobind was somewhat hot-tempered, and spoke harshly to the Pathans, the result of which was that he was put in prison with his family. In the end he obtained his release by abandoning his own religion, and, along with his family, becoming a Mussulman.

Ramgobind Ghosal and his family got home with their lives, it is true, but, being Mussulmans, they were utterly outcasted by their own society. At this time Nobokumar's father was alive, and he accordingly had to abandon the outcast daughter-in-law along with her outcast father. So it was that Nobokumar never knew his wife.

Abandoned by his kinsmen, an outcast from society, Ramgobind Ghosal could not remain long in his own society. Partly for this reason, and partly from a desire for promotion through the king's favour, he went with his family to the capital Rajmahal, and began to reside there. He and his family had adopted Mohammedan names along with their change of religion. What became of his father-in-law or his wife, after they had gone to Rajmahal, Nobokumar had no means of knowing, and up to this time did not know anything. From disappointment, Nobokumar did not marry again, and this is why I have said that Nobokumar had not even one wife.

The Adhikari was not aware of all this. He thought, "What harm is there in a Kulin having two wives?" He said openly to Nobokumar, "I came to ask you something. This girl who has saved your life has ruined herself for another's benefit. The great man under whose care she lives is of a terrible disposition; and if she returns to him, she will fare as you were about to. Can you suggest any remedy for this?"

Nobokumar sat up, and said, "I too was anxious on that account. You know everything, do you devise some remedy. If I can benefit her by giving up my life, I am willing even to do that. I am determined to return and give myself up to that murderer; by doing so I shall save her life. The Adhikari laughed and said, "You are a fool. What will be the good of that? You too will be killed, while the great man's resentment towards her will not in any way be diminished. There is but one remedy for this."

Nob. What is that?

Adhi. For her to flee with you. But that is very difficult. If you remain with me, you will be captured in a day or two. The great man constantly visits this temple: so that I see misfortune in store for Kopal-Kundala.

Nobokumar eagerly asked, "What is the difficulty in her fleeing with me?"

Adhi. You do not know whose daughter she is, or from what family sprung, whose wife, or what her character. Will you make her your companion, and, if you take her with you, will you give her a shelter in your own home? And if you don't do so, where is the orphan to go to?

Nobokumar pondered for a moment, and

said, "Nothing is impossible to me for the sake of my life's preserver. She shall remain with me as my wife."

Adhi. Good; but when your kinsmen and relatives ask you whose wife she is, what will you say? Nobokumar again thought, and said, "Do you tell me all about her, and I will tell them that."

Adhi. Good; but, on the other hand, how can a young man and a young woman go alone together? What will people say? How will you explain the matter to your kinsfolk and relatives? And I, who call this girl mother, how am I to send her alone to a distant country with a young man of whose character I know nothing?"

The king of ghataks[1] was not a bad hand in his profession.

Nobokumar said, "Come with us."

Adhi. I go with you! Then who will perform the worship of Bhobani?

[1] A *ghatak* is a sort of marriage-monger or broker, who arranges marriages, and gets a fee from both sides. He is supposed to know the history and genealogy of different families.

Nobokumar was vexed, and said, "Well then, can't you hit upon some plan?"

Adhi. There is only one plan, and that depends on your noble-mindedness.

Nob. What is that? I will consent to anything. Tell me your plan.

Adhi. Listen. This girl is a Brahman's daughter. I know all about her history. She was kidnapped in her infancy by cruel Christian pirates, and, being shipwrecked, they abandoned her on this seashore. She will tell you all about that hereafter. The Kapálik got hold of her, and was bringing her up for the accomplishment of his vows; and in no long time he would have succeeded in his purpose. The girl is yet a virgin, and her character is thoroughly pure. Do you marry her, and take her to your home. No one will be able to say anything, for I will marry you according to the Shastres.

Nobokumar started up from his bed, and hastily began to walk to and fro. As he made no reply, the Adhikari waited a moment, and said, "Go to sleep now; to-morrow morning I will arouse you. If you like, you can go alone; I will put you on the road to Midnapur. So saying the Adhikari took leave: as he went he muttered to himself, "Can it be that I have forgotten the *ghatkali* of my native land?"

CHAPTER IX.

IN THE HOUSE OF GOD.

At morning the Adhikari came to Nobokumar's side, and saw that even now he was not asleep. He asked him what was to be done. Nobokumar said, "From to-day Kopal-Kundala is my holy wife. For her sake I will forsake the world, if necessary. Who will give away the maiden?"

The face of the star of ghataks expanded with joy. He thought, "After so long a time by the mercy of Juggadumba my goddess has found a way." Then he said, "I will give her away."

The Adhikari again entered his own bed-chamber. He had some very worn and faded palm-leaves in a box, on which were written his lunar days, stars, &c. He examined them all carefully, and came back and said, "Though to-day is not a marriage-day, still there is no obstacle to marriage. I will give away the girl at evening.[1] To-day you will simply remain fasting, and when you get home you can perform all the ceremonies customary in your family. I have a place to conceal you in for one day. If he comes to-day, he will not be able to find you. To-morrow, after the marriage, go home with your wife."

Nobokumar agreed to this. The ceremony was performed, as far as the circumstances permitted, in accordance with the Shastres; at evening Nobokumar was married to the young Kapálik-nurtured devotee.

There was no news of the Kapálik. The next morning all three prepared to start, as the Adhikari was to put them on the road to Midnapur. Before starting Kopal-Kundala went to make her obeisance to Káli. Having

[1] The word for evening in the original is a word meaning "the dust of cows," *i.e.* the time when cows, returning from the grazing-ground, stir up dust with their feet.

bowed low with reverence, she took an entire bael-leaf from a vessel of flowers, and placed it at the feet of the image, and intently watched it. The leaf fell down.

Kopal-Kundala was exceedingly superstitious. Seeing the bael-leaf fall down from the feet of the image she was alarmed, and told the Adhikari. He, too, was grieved, and said, "It is too late to go back; now your husband only is your religion. If your husband goes to the burying-ground,[1] you will have to go with him. So go quietly."

All went quietly. Very late they arrived at the Midnapur road, and there the Adhikari took leave of them. Kopal-Kundala began to cry. She was taking leave of the one good friend she had in the world.

[1] This refers to the practice of suttee, which was abolished by a law passed during the viceroyalty of Lord Bentinck. At the present time the Hindoos regard such a practice with horror, though at the time the opposition to the bill was most keen and determined, and it was said the measure was only the prelude to a systematic scheme for the destruction of the Hindoo religion. As Bentham has well remarked, "Morality and legislation have the same centre, though not the same circumference. Morality quickly follows in the footsteps of legislation."

The Adhikari, too, began to cry. Wiping away his tears, he whispered to Kopal-Kundala, "Mother! you know that, by God's favour, your child has plenty of money. All in Hidgellee, high and low, worship through him. Give your husband what I have tied in your cloth, and tell him to get a palki for you. Think of me as your child."

With these words the Adhikari went away weeping; Kopal-Kundala, too, went on her way weeping.

END OF THE FIRST PART.

PART II.

CHAPTER I.

ON THE HIGH ROAD.

SOME writer has said that man's life is but a poem. One canto of Kopal-Kundala's life-poem had passed. What was to follow ?

On arriving at Midnapur, Nobokumar engaged a female servant, a guard, and some palki-bearers for Kopal-Kundala with the Adhikari's money ; and putting her in the palki, he sent her on. For want of money, he himself went on foot. Nobokumar was weary with the former day's toil, and after the mid-day meal the bearers left him far behind. Gradually evening came on, and the sky was covered with the fleecy clouds of cold weather. Evening passed away, and the world became dark. A little rain, too, began to fall. Nobokumar felt anxious to catch up Kopal-Kundala, and he felt certain that he would see her at the first serai,[1] but no serai was yet in sight. About four or six *dandas* of the night had passed, and Nobokumar began to run, when suddenly his foot struck against some hard substance, which broke with a crackling sound under his tread. Nobokumar stood still. He again moved his feet, and again the same sound. He took the substance up in his hands, and saw that it was like a piece of broken plank.

Though the sky was covered with clouds, it had not become so very dark that the shape of a large thing could not be seen in an open place. In front lay something large. Nobokumar perceived that it was a broken palki, and at once fear for Kopal-Kundala's safety

[1] *Serai*, a staging-house on a road. The Mohammedan emperors built a number of such serais along the principal lines of communication and pilgrim routes. Under British rule they have fallen somewhat into neglect and disrepair, except in municipalities. But private serais or lodging-houses are springing up everywhere, at which accommodation can be had for a very moderate price.

leapt to his heart. Going towards the palki, his foot struck against a different sort of substance. The touch appeared to be like that of a tender human body. Sitting down and spreading his hand over it, he saw that it was a human body. It was very cold to the touch, and at the same time he felt something liquid. Feeling the pulse, he perceived that there was no movement, and that life had left the body. But listening with great attention, it seemed as if he could hear the sound of inward and outward breathing. If there is breath, then why no pulse? Is it a sick man? Putting his hand to the nostrils, he perceived that no breath was coming out. Then why was there a sound? It may be that there is also some live person here. Thinking this, he asked, "Is there any live person here?"

A soft voice replied, "I am."

Nobokumar said, "Who are you?" The answer was "Who are you?" In Nobokumar's ear the voice sounded like that of a woman's. So he eagerly asked, "Is it Kopal-Kundala?"

The woman replied, "I don't know who Kopal-Kundala is; I have just been robbed of my *kundalas*."[1]

Hearing a joke, Nobokumar was a little cheered. He asked, "What has happened?"

The speaker replied, "Robbers have broken my palki, and have killed one of my bearers. The others have run away. The robbers have stripped me of my ornaments, and have tied me in the palki."

Nobokumar could perceive in the darkness that a woman was really tied firmly in the palki with a cloth. He quickly loosened the fastening, and said, "Can you get up?"

The woman said, "One blow of a stick struck me also. I feel a pain in my foot, but I think that I could rise with a little help."

Nobokumar stretched out his arm, by the aid of which the woman got up. Nobokumar said, "Will you be able to walk?"

The woman gave no reply, but asked,

[1] *Kundalas* = ear-rings. The joke or pun in the original lies in the word *niskundala*, which means "deprived of ear-rings."

"Have you seen whether any traveller is coming along behind you?"

Nobokumar replied in the negative.

The woman again asked, "How far is the *chuttee?*"[1]

Nobokumar said, "I can't say, but it must be close at hand."

The woman said, "How am I to sit in the fields alone with you in the darkness; I must go with you to the *chuttee.* I think I can walk, if I had something to lean upon."

Nobokumar said, "It is folly to be modest at a time of danger. Lean on my shoulder."

The woman was not foolish. So she went along leaning on Nobokumar's shoulder.

As a matter of fact, the *chuttee* was quite close. At that time robbers did not fear to commit crimes of violence quite close to

[1] A *chuttee* is a serai and something more. It is a small cluster of houses (comprising a shop or two), which springs up on much-frequented routes to supply the wants of pilgrims and others using the road. If the road be much frequented and the *chuttee* be three miles or more from the nearest village on either side, a liquor shop will generally be found there, or in North Behar, a ganja shop, or in Orissa, an opium shop.

chuttees. In a short time Nobokumar arrived there with his companion.

Nobokumar saw that Kopal-Kundala was in the *chuttee,* her male and female servant having prepared a house for her. Nobokumar quickly engaged a house close to it for his companion, and placed her in it. At his order the landlord's wife brought a light. When the rays of the light fell on his companion's body, Nobokumar saw that she was uncommonly beautiful. The full bloom of her youth was overflowing with the waves of her beauty, like a river in the month of Srabun.

CHAPTER II.

IN THE HOUSE BY THE ROAD.

If this woman had been a faultless beauty, then I could have said, "Reader! she is as beautiful as your wife;[1] and, fair reader! she is as lovely as the reflection in your mirror!" In so many words, the description would have been complete. But, unfortunately, I must abstain from such a description, as she was not perfect in every feature and limb.

The reason why I saw she was not a faultless beauty is that, in the first place, her body was somewhat taller than middle-height;

[1] Bengalees are married by their parents when children, or quite young, and therefore do not choose their own wives. It is therefore all the more surprising that they should be so thoroughly satisfied with their wives, and consider them combinations of Venus and Minerva. Bengalees are often the devoted slaves of their wives, and there is far more petticoat government in Bengal than is generally supposed.

secondly, her lips were a trifle broad; and thirdly, her colour was not fair, in the true sense of the word.

She was rather tall, it is true, but her arms, legs, breast, and in fact all her limbs, were well-rounded and well-developed. Just as in the rains a creeper trembles under the weight of its own leaves, so her frame trembled with its own ripeness; and for this reason her somewhat lofty stature derived an additional beauty from her full development. Of those whom I call really fair-coloured, some resemble the moonlight of the full moon, others again are like the rosy-faced dawn. Her colour was neither of these, and though for this reason I have said she was not really fair, still her complexion was not deficient in fascinating power. She was of a brown[1] colour; not the dark

[1] It is impossible to translate adequately the word in the vernacular. The variety of complexions among the Bengalees is scarcely less than the variety of castes. We meet with the jet black, creamy white, turmeric yellow, burnished gold, copper red, lemon, bamboo, chocolate, coffee, and a hundred gradual variations of these colours. The colour referred to in the text is something between, or a combination produced by black, molten lead, coffee, and indigo.

colour by which Sham's mother and Shamsoonder[1] are depicted, but the rich brown colour of molten gold. If the rays of the full moon, on the dawn crowned with golden clouds, represent the colour of fair-limbed women, then the colour I am describing may be compared to the beauty of the new mango-leaves that come out in spring. Many of my readers may praise light-coloured women, but the man who is fascinated by such a brown cannot be said to be devoid of the sense of colour. If any one disagrees with what I say, then let him for a moment think of the tresses hanging over that bright brown forehead, like a cluster of bees seated on young mango leaves; let him contemplate the eye-brows touching the curls under that forehead, resembling the moon of the seventh day; let him think of those cheeks, purple as the ripe mango; and between the cheeks let him regard those small deep-red lips,—if he does

[1] Shamsoonder, *i.e.* the god Krishna, who is always represented as having a bluish-black skin. In Orissa the upper castes are very fond of blue *dhotees* (waist-cloths), blue being Krishna's colour.

this, he will feel that this unknown woman is the queen of beauties. Her eyes were not very large, but they had well-curved lids, and were very bright. Her glance was steady and penetrating. If she looked at you, you would feel at that moment that this woman is reading your heart. As you look, that penetrating glance assumes a different character, and the eyes melt in a tender, loving gaze; while now and again appears nothing but an expression of fatigue caused by a surfeit of pleasure, as if the eyes were a couch for the dreams of Cupid; sometimes opening with desire, and quivering with the juice of love, and again flashing a cruel glance from the corner of her eye, like flashes of lightning in the clouds! The loveliness of her face had two indescribable beauties; the first derived from the splendour of an all-penetrating intellect, and the second from a majestic self-respect. For these reasons when she stood up curving her swan's throat, you might easily suppose her to be the queen of the race of women.

The fair one's age was twenty-seven—the

overflowing river of the month of Bhadro.[1] Like the river-water in Bhadro, her wealth of beauty was surging and overflowing. More than her colour, more than her eyes, more than all was the flashing fascination of that beauty. Her whole frame was constantly quivering with the weight of her ripe youth, as, when there is no breeze, a river quivers in the young autumn; and this quivering changefulness each moment added a fresh lustre to her beauty. Nobokumar was steadily gazing at this ever-fresh beauty.

The fair one, seeing Nobokumar's thirsty gaze, said, "What are you looking at?"

Nobokumar was a gentleman; being somewhat confounded, he bent down his head. Seeing him at a loss for a reply, the unknown one again said with a smile, "Have you never seen a woman, or do you think me very beautiful?"

If these words had been spoken in a natural tone they would have appeared like a rebuke,

[1] Bhadro = the latter half of August and the first half of September, when the rivers are in full flood.

but the smile which accompanied them showed that the woman spoke in fun. Nobokumar saw that she was very pert, and why should he not answer a pert woman's question? So he said, "I have seen women, but I have never seen so beautiful a woman."

The woman asked with some pride, "Not a single one?" Kopal-Kundala's beauty was awake in Nobokumar's heart, so he too replied with some pride, "I cannot go so far as to say not a single one."

The blow of iron fell on the stone. The speaker said, "Good; is she your wife?"

Nob. Why? Why do you think it is my wife?

The Woman. Bengalees always think their wives are more beautiful than anybody else.

Nob. I am a Bengali. You too speak like a Bengali; of what country are you?"

The young woman looked at her clothes and said, "This unfortunate one is not a Bengali; she is an up-country Mussulman." Nobokumar scanned her, and saw that in truth her dress was like that of an up-country Mussulman woman. After a moment, the woman said—

"Sir, by your skilful questions you have found me out; now satisfy my curiosity by telling me who you are. Where is the house in which that unrivalled beauty resides?"

Nobokumar said, "I live at Septogram."

The foreigner made no reply, but quickly held down her head, and began to make the light brighter.[1]

After a moment she said, without raising her head, "Your slave's name is Moti; am I not to hear your name?"

Nobokumar said, "Nobokumar Sarma."

The light went out.

[1] The light is a wick placed in a small vessel of oil. To conceal her interest or agitation, Moti Bibi began to push the wick further into the oil. Not that she wanted more light, but the action occupied her restless hands, and enabled her to conceal her face.

CHAPTER III.

THE MEETING OF THE BEAUTIES.

NOBOKUMAR called the woman of the house, and told her to bring another light. Before it was brought, he heard the sound of a deep sigh. A moment after the light was brought a Mussulman, in the garb of a servant, appeared. The up-country woman seeing him, said, "What is this? why have you been so long? Where are all the others?"

The servant said, "The bearers were drunk, and in getting them together I fell behind the palki. After that, on seeing a broken palki and not seeing you, I utterly lost my senses. Some of them are there, and some have gone in different directions to look for you. I have come here in search of you."

Moti said, "Bring them here."

The servant made a salaam and went away. The foreign woman remained sitting for sometime with her face in her hands.

Nobokumar asked leave to go. Then Moti rose as one from a dream, and asked in the same tone as before, "Where are you going to stop?"

Nob. In the house next to this.

Moti. I saw a palki near the house; is anybody with you?

Nob. My wife is with me.

Moti Bibi again got an opportunity for jesting, and said, "What, is she the peerless beauty?"

Nob. If you see her, you will know.

Moti. Is she to be seen?

Nob. (thoughtfully) Why not?

Moti. Then do me a favour. I am exceedingly anxious to see an unequalled beauty. I want to go to Agra and mention her. But not now; go away now, and in a little while I will send you word.

Nobokumar went away. After a few moments, many male and female servants and bearers came up, bringing boxes and other things. A palki, too, arrived, inside which was a female servant. Then word was brought to Nobokumar that the lady had sent for him.

Nobokumar returned to Moti Bibi. He saw that this time her beauty was different. Moti Bibi had taken off the dress she had been wearing, and had decked herself out with ornaments and embroidered robes, sparkling with gold, pearls, and other precious stones. The unornamented body she had adorned with ornaments. In all that she had on, everywhere diamonds and other gems were sparkling out from the gold,—on her hair, hair-knot, on her forehead, by her eyes, in her ears, on her throat, breast, and arms. Nobokumar's eyes were dazzled. An over-abundance of gold ornaments rather detracts from the beauty of most women; many look just like dressed-up dolls. But Moti Bibi had not that appearance, nor was her beauty lessened. The abundance of ornaments appeared to be in harmony with her somewhat large body, like the sky adorned with large constellations, and her beauty was thereby enhanced. Moti Bibi said to Nobokumar, "Come along, sir, let me be introduced to your wife."

Nobokumar took Moti Bibi with him. The servant, who had come in the palki, also accompanied them. Her name was Pesmon.

Kopal-Kundala was sitting alone on the damp floor of the shop. Only a small light was burning; her thick unconfined tresses darkened her back. When Moti Bibi first saw her, a slight smile could be seen on the corner of her lip and in her eyes. In order to see better, she took up the light and brought it near Kopal-Kundala's face. Then her smiles disappeared, and Moti's face became grave. She gazed on her with unflinching eyes. Neither one spoke a word; Moti was fascinated, and Kopal-Kundala somewhat astonished.

After a moment or two Moti began to take off the ornaments from her limbs. She undid them all, and one by one commenced to put them on Kopal-Kundala. Kopal-Kundala did not say a word. Nobokumar said, "What are you doing there?" but Moti gave no reply.

Having finished covering her with ornaments, Moti said to Nobokumar, "You spoke the truth. This flower does not bloom even in the gardens of kings. The pity of it is that I cannot exhibit this wealth of beauty at the capital. These ornaments suit her limbs—for this reason I have put them on her. You too must sometimes put them on her and think of the forward foreign lady."

Nobokumar was astounded, and said, "What! those priceless ornaments. I cannot take them."

Moti said, "By the grace of God I have others; I shall not be deprived of all my ornaments. If I feel a pleasure in letting her wear them, why should you thwart me?"

So saying, Moti Bibi went away with her handmaid. When they were alone, Pesmon asked Moti Bibi, "My lady, who is this man?"

The young Mussulmanee replied, "My husband!"

CHAPTER IV.

THE PALKI JOURNEY.

LISTEN to what became of the ornaments. Moti Bibi had sent an ivory box inlaid with silver for keeping the ornaments. The robbers had only taken a few of her things; they succeeded in taking nothing except what was actually with her.

Nobokumar left one or two ornaments on Kopal-Kundala's body, and put the greater portion in the box. The next morning Moti Bibi started for Burdwan, while Nobokumar and his wife started in the direction of Septogram. Nobokumar put Kopal-Kundala in the palki, and placed the box of jewels with her. The bearers easily left Nobokumar behind. Kopal-Kundala opened the doors of the palki, and went along looking in every direction.

A beggar saw her and ran along by the side of the palki asking for alms.

Kopal-Kundala said, "I have nothing; what can I give you?"

The beggar pointed to the few ornaments Kopal-Kundala had on, and said, "What, mother! There are diamonds and pearls on your body, and you say you have nothing?"

Kopal-Kundala said, "Will you be satisfied with the ornaments?"

The beggar was a little astonished; a beggar's hopes are unbounded. After a moment she replied, "Of course I shall be satisfied."

In the innocence of her heart Kopal-Kundala gave the beggar the ornaments, box and all. She also took off and gave her the ornaments she was wearing.

The beggar stood confused for a moment. The male and female servant had seen nothing. The hesitation of the beggar was but momentary. She looked in all directions, and hastily ran away with the ornaments. Kopal-Kundala wondered why the beggar had run away.

CHAPTER V.

IN ONE'S NATIVE COUNTRY.

NOBOKUMAR arrived with Kopal-Kundala in his own country. His father was dead, and his widow-mother and two sisters were in the house. The elder was a widow; the reader will see nothing of her. The second, Shamasoondri, was a widow, though married—in a word, she was a Kulin's wife; we shall now and then see something of her.

If under any other circumstances Nobokumar had married and brought home a young devotee of unknown family and temperament, I cannot say how far his relatives and friends would have been pleased. But, as a matter of fact, he had no trouble on this score. All had despaired of his return. His comrades had returned and given out that Nobokumar had been killed by tigers. The reader will think that these truth-tellers spoke to what they considered certain; but to admit this would be to insult their powers of imagination. Many of the returned pilgrims had positively declared that with their own eyes they had seen Nobokumar fall into a tiger's jaws; sometimes there would be a discussion as to the size of the tiger. Some said it must be eight cubits in length, while others swore it was nearly fourteen cubits. The old pilgrim, to whom we have been introduced above, said, "However that may be, I had a very narrow escape. The tiger had made for me, when I fled; Nobokumar is not so bold a man, and couldn't run away."

On all these rumours reaching the ears of Nobokumar's relatives, such a crying and weeping arose in the house, that for several days it did not cease. On hearing the news of the death of her only son, Nobokumar's mother became like one quite dead. Such being the juncture at which Nobokumar arrived at home with his wife, who was likely to ask him what caste or whose daughter his bride was? All were blind with joy. Nobokumar's mother received her daughter-in-law with great respect and affection.

When Nobokumar saw that Kopal-Kundala was affectionately received in his house, the sea of his joy overflowed. Though he had won Kopal-Kundala, he had hitherto manifested no signs of joy or love through fear of her being ill-received; still the sky of his heart was overspread with the image of Kopal-Kundala. It was owing to this uncertainty that he had not at once consented to the proposal to marry Kopal-Kundala; and for the same reason on the way home he had had no loving conversation with Kopal-Kundala, though he was her husband. He did not allow the waves to be tossed about in a sea of love about to overflow. But that uncertainty vanished; just as a heap of water rushes with terrific force on the removal of some boulder that has held it back, with such force did the sea of Nobokumar's love overflow.

This uprising of love did not always manifest itself in words, but it could be seen in the moist eyes with which Nobokumar used to gaze at Kopal-Kundala; it could be seen in the way in which he would feign some necessity, though there was really none, for coming to Kopal-Kundala's side; it could be seen in the manner in which he would abruptly turn the conversation on Kopal-Kundala; it even showed itself in his absent walk; it could be seen in his eagerness day and night to study Kopal-Kundala's happiness. His whole nature seemed to change. Gravity took the place of flippancy, and sadness gave way to cheerfulness. Nobokumar's face was always cheerful. As his heart was a receptacle for love, his love for all others increased; his annoyance with those who vexed him was less; everybody became the object of his love. It appeared to him that the world had been created for good deeds only, and the whole earth appeared beautiful. Such is love! Love softens the harsh, makes the wicked good, the unholy holy, darkness light.

And Kopal-Kundala? What were her feelings? Come, reader, we will take a look at her.

CHAPTER VI.

IN THE FEMALE APARTMENTS.

It is well known that in former times Septogram was a city of great wealth. At one time the merchants of every country from Java to Constantinople used to collect in that great city for commerce; but in the tenth or eleventh century of the Bengal era the pristine magnificence of Septogram declined. The principal reason for the decline lay in the fact that the river, which used to wash past the outskirts of the city, had now become a narrow stream, so that ships of large burden could no longer come up to the city. For this reason its extensive trade gradually disappeared. When a commercial city loses its commerce, it loses everything: Septogram lost everything. In the eleventh century

Hooghly, with its newly acquired grandeur, began to rival it, and the Portuguese set on foot a trade which was gradually dragging the goddess of wealth away from Septogram. But even then Septogram had not altogether lost its former magnificence; it was still the residence of the Foujdar and other royal Ministers. However, a large portion of the city had become poor and depopulated, and now resembled a mere hamlet.

Nobokumar's house was in a desolate suburb of Septogram, which was now very little frequented in the present shattered fortunes of the city. The roads were overgrown with creepers and shrubs, and behind Nobokumar's house was a dense extensive forest. In front of it, at a distance of about two miles, flowed a small stream, which, after skirting a small jungle, entered the forest behind the house. The house was made of brick, and was not a bad-sized house for that period and place. It was two-storeyed, but not very high. At the present time many one-storeyed houses are as high.

Two young girls were standing on the terrace of this house, and enjoying the view. It was evening; the outlook on all sides was enchanting. On one side, close by, was a dense forest, in which countless birds were singing; on the opposite side a small stream lay like a silver thread. At a distance sparkled the countless terraced roofs of the city, full of townsmen eager to quaff the spring breezes. In another direction, some distance away, twilight was gradually deepening down on the broad bosom of the Bhagirutti, adorned with boats.

Of the two young women standing on the terrace, the complexion of one was like the rays of the moonlight; she was half-concealed by her masses of unconfined hair. The other was dark, beautiful, and sixteen. Her body and face were both small. The upper portion of her face was encircled with tiny black curls, as the leaves of the blue lotus encircle the lotus flower. Her eyes were large, and of a tender white colour, like the *saphri* fish. Her fingers were very small, and buried in the waves of her companion's hair. The reader has understood that the girl with the complexion of moonlight was Kopal-Kundala; and I will inform him that the dark one was her husband's sister,[1] Shamasoondri.

Shamasoondri sometimes called her brother's wife "Bo,"[2] and sometimes affectionately "Bon," and sometimes "Mrino." The name of Kopal-Kundala being terribly long, the family had nicknamed her "Mrinomoi;" hence the title "Mrino." We too shall sometimes call her Mrinomoi.

Shamasoondri was repeating a bit of poetry she had learnt as a child. She said, "Will you alone remain a devotee?"

Mrinomoi replied, "Why, am I doing any penance?"

Shamasoondri, lifting Mrinomoi's waves of hair with her hands, said, "Aren't you going to do up your masses of hair?"

[1] The Bengalees have a different word for husband's sister (*nonod*) and wife's sister (*bhouj*). The *nonod* is often inimical to the *bhouj*, and the feeling between them corresponds to the proverbial feeling between mothers-in-law and sons-in-law in England.

[2] "Bo" = daughter-in-law. Kopal-Kundala was the daughter-in-law of the house.

Mrinomoi only smiled and pulled her hair away from Shamasoondri's hand.

Shamasoondri again said, "Well, do what I wish, and for once dress yourself like us grihusti[1] women. How long will you remain an ascetic?"

Mri. I was an ascetic before I had seen this Brahman youth.

Sha. You must be one no longer.

Mri. Why not?

Sha. Why? d'you wish to see? I will break your asceticism. Do you know what they call the touchstone?

Mrinomoi said, "No."

Sha. The touchstone turns even copper into gold.

Mri. What of that?

Sha. Women also have their touchstone.

Mri. What is that?

Sha. Man. By the breath of man even the

[1] Grihusti woman means a respectable female member of a respectable family. Even a widow living alone may be spoken of as *grihusti*, in contradistinction to *ghusgi*, which means a woman of somewhat loose morals.

Jogini[1] is changed into the *Grihini*.[2] You have touched that stone, you will see.

"I will tie up your masses of hair, I will put fine clothes on you,
I will hang flowers from your top-knot;
I will put the *sithi*[3] on your forehead, on your waist the *chandrahar*,[3]
And a pair of ear-rings in your ears.
I will give you saffron, sandal, myrrh, and plates of pán and betel-nut.
Your face will be red in colour.
I will place in your lap a gold doll-child,
And see if you like it or not."

Mrinomoi said, "Well, I understand. Suppose I have touched the touchstone, and have become gold: I tie up my hair, I wear

[1] *Jogini*, a female ascetic.

[2] *Grihini*, the mistress or matron of a household, often spoken of as "*Ginni*."

[3] *Sithi*, also called *simontini*, an ornament which is worn along the parting at the top of the head, and stretches along the edge of the forehead on either side to the ears. *Chandrahar* is a silver waist-belt. The ornaments of Bengali women are numerous and varied. Perhaps the commonest way of investing savings is to spend it on ornaments for the wife or other female members of the family. The gold used is pure, so that the ornaments, when sold, realise almost as much as they cost, whereas English ornaments rarely realise more than twenty per cent. of their cost price. It may be said that the end-all and be-all of a Bengali woman's existence is to wear

fine clothes, I put flowers in my hair-knot, a *chandrahar* on my waist, and ear-rings in my ears. Sandal, saffron, myrrh, pan, betel-nut and gold doll,—I have them all. I have them all, mind you; but admitting all this, what happiness have I?"

Sha. Tell me, what pleasure has the flower in blooming?

Mri. Those who see it experience pleasure; but what pleasure has the flower?

Shamasoondri's face became grave; her eyes shook a little like a blue lotus struck by the

as many ornaments as possible. When they pay visits, they often borrow ornaments from their female friends. The lower castes, who cannot afford gold or silver, wear brass, bell-metal, zinc, &c. The Ooria women wear large brass ornaments which cover their arms from the wrist to the elbow. In this and other matters of taste and perception, the Ooria lags far behind the Bengali. But Bengali women are by no means of opinion that beauty when unadorned is adorned the most! Their ambition is to possess a complete set of ornaments. For instance, there are no fewer than six different sorts of bracelets for the wrist, as *churi*, *bala*, &c. Then there are six different armlets worn above the elbow, *e.g.*, *tabiz*, *bazu*, *ananta*, &c. The prettiest ornament is the gold *chik* or necklace. The ears are pierced in three places, at the top, at the bottom, and in the middle. Then there are various sorts of waistlets and anklets, and rings on the fingers and toes. Love of ornaments may be called an important factor for evil or for good in Bengali social life.

morning wind. She said, "What pleasure has the flower? That I cannot say. I have never been a flower and bloomed; but had I been a bud like you, then I should have found pleasure in blooming."

Shama was the wife of a Kulin.[1]

[1] This means that Shama never or scarcely ever was blessed with the sight of her husband. Large sums are paid by fathers of girls for Kulin bridegrooms. A Kulin Brahman girl, to preserve her caste and social position intact, must be married to a Kulin bridegroom. So it happens that Kulin youths are sometimes married to ten or twenty different wives. They can visit the houses of their numerous fathers-in-law, and are not only well entertained when there, but expect a present on coming away. There have been cases in which poor fathers of Kulin girls have taken them and had them wedded to old men on the point of death. They cannot afford to pay for a young and suitable bridegroom, and it is an indelible disgrace for their daughters to remain unmarried. On the other hand, Brahmans of lower family have to pay for a bride, and a Piroli or a Bhuttacharjya may reach the age of thirty-five before he can afford to marry. The state of things is not so bad as it used to be. The feeling of the upper classes of Hindoos is strongly in favour of monogamy, and a Kulin who marries many wives is regarded with some contempt and aversion. For instance, a Kulin weds the daughter of a rich Tagore (Piroli) family. The wife is the mistress and probably remains on in her father's house. The husband falls into the position of a sort of paid retainer and loses respect and dignity. Even among the Mussulmans one wife is the rule. In case of barrenness, or misconduct of the first wife, a second wife is married *nika*. But, in the absence of sufficient cause, the man who inflicts a *sotin* (co-wife) on his first wife is considered worthy of blame.

We will take this opportunity of informing the reader that a flower feels pleasure in blooming; its pleasure consists in the bestowal of its juice and fragrance. Giving and receiving are the bases of all pleasure: there is no third basis. Mrinomoi, from living in the wilds, had never realised this, therefore she made no reply.

Shamasoondri, observing her silence, said, "Well, if this is not so, then tell me in what does your pleasure consist?"

Mrinomoi thought for a little, and said, "I cannot say. I think I should be happy if I could wander about in those forests by the sea-shore."

Shamasoondri was a little astonished. She was also somewhat vexed that Mrinomoi had not benefited by their care. She was a little angry also, and said, "Have you any means of going back now?"

Mri. No.

Shama. Then what will you do?

Mri. The Adhikari used to say, "Destiny must be fulfilled."

Shamasoondri put her face in her cloth, and said, laughing, "Certainly, Mr. Bhuttacharjya,[1] what is all that?"

Mrinomoi heaved a sigh and said, "I will do whatever the Creator causes me to do; whatever is in my fate must come to pass."

Sha. Why, whatever is in your fate? There is happiness in your fate. Why do you sigh so deeply?

Mrinomoi said, "Listen. On the day I set out with my husband, just before starting I went to place three leaves at Bhobani's feet. I never used to do anything without placing three leaves at the mother's lotus feet. If the undertaking was to be successful, the mother used to accept the three leaves; if there was likely to be any disaster, the leaves used to fall. I felt some hesitation in coming with an unknown man to an unknown country; I went to the mother to know what was

[1] Mrinomoi had spoken in Sanskrit, so Shamasoondri jokingly calls her Bhuttacharjya, that is, a Brahman who teaches Sanskrit in a small *tole* or school.

fitting. The mother did not accept the three leaves, so I cannot say what is in store for me."

Mrinomoi remained silent; Shamasoondri shuddered.

END OF PART II.

PART III.

CHAPTER I.

IN THE PAST.

WHEN Nobokumar started with Kopal-Kundala from the *chuttee*, Moti Bibi went by another road to Burdwan. While she is on her way, we will say something of her former history. Moti's character was very corrupt, but at the same time she had many good qualities. The reader will not object to a more detailed account of such a character.

When her father embraced the Mohammedan religion, her Hindoo name was changed into Lutufonissa; Moti Bibi was never her name, but she used to take it whenever she travelled incognita in different countries. Her father went to Dacca, and got an appointment under the emperor. But there were many of his own countrypeople there, and no one, after being outcasted, likes to remain in the same society. For this reason, he for some time gained favour in the eyes of the Subadar, and getting letters from many of his Minister friends, he came to Agra with his family. No one's merits remained concealed from Akber Shah, who was not slow to appreciate his worth. Lutufonissa's father was quickly promoted to a high post, and was reckoned as one of the principal nobles of Agra. In the meanwhile Lutufonissa was gradually growing up. On coming to Agra, she was well instructed in Persian, Sanskrit, dancing, singing, wit, and other accomplishments. She began to be reckoned among the countless beautiful and virtuous ladies of the capital; but, unfortunately, she had not been so well instructed in morals as in secular education. When Lutufonissa grew up, it became clear that the inclinations of her mind were quite unrestrainable; she had neither power nor wish to curb her passions. Her inclinations for good or evil were alike; she never used to consider before doing anything, that this action is a good one, and that a bad one; she used to do whatever pleased her. If a good action gave her pleasure, she would do it, and *vice versâ.* The sins which spring from the strength of youthful passions were produced in Lutufonissa. As her former husband was living, none of the nobles were willing to marry her; nor was she particularly desirous of marrying. Why, thought she, should she clip the wings of the bee that sports from flower to flower? At first things were whispered about her, and at last her corruption became a matter of common talk. Her father got angry, and turned her out of his house.

Among those on whom Lutufonissa used secretly to bestow her favours, was the young Prince Selim. The latter had not yet made Lutufonissa an inmate of his harem, through fear of incurring the wrath of his impartial sire by bringing dishonour on a noble's family. Now there was a good opportunity. The sister of the Rajput chief, Mán Singh, was the Prince's chief consort. The Prince made Lutufonissa her head companion. In the eyes of the world, Lutufonissa was the Begum's friend, but in secret the Prince's concubine.

It may easily be imagined that a clever woman like Lutufonissa would quickly captivate the Prince's heart; her ascendency over Selim was so unrivalled, that she determined, when a fitting opportunity presented itself, to become his queen. Nor was such resolve entirely confined to Lutufonissa, for all the inmates of the palace looked upon it as probable. In the dream of such a hope Lutufonissa was passing her life, when she was rudely awakened. Meheronissa, the daughter of Khaja Ayas, Akber Shah's treasurer, was the queen of Mussulman beauties. One day the Treasurer invited Selim and other men of note to his house. There Selim first met Meheronissa, and was captivated by her. What happened after that is known to all readers of history. The Treasurer's daughter had already been betrothed to one Sher Afghan by name, a very brave noble. Selim, blind with love, asked his father to cancel the betrothal, but he only received a rebuke from his just sire. Therefore Selim had to desist for the present; but though he desisted for the present, he did not give up all hope. Meheronissa was married to Sher Afghan. But Selim's desires were in the mirror of Lutufonissa's nails; she clearly saw that there was no escape for Sher Afghan, not if he had a thousand lives. When Akber Shah died, his life also would be put an end to, and Meheronissa would become Selim's queen. Lutufonissa gave up all hopes of the throne.

The life of Akber, the glory of Mohammedan emperors, came to an end. That brilliant sun, whose splendour had lighted up all countries from Turkey to the Brahmaputra,—that sun set. At this juncture, Lutufonissa resolved upon a desperate plan for maintaining her own ascendency.

The Rajput chief, Raja Mán Singh's sister, was Selim's chief queen. Khasru was her son. One day Lutufonissa was talking with her about Akber Shah's illness, and was congratulating the Rajput girl on soon becoming the Emperor's wife, to which Khasru's mother replied, "It is true one's birth is successful, if one becomes the Emperor's wife; but she who is the mother of the Emperor, she is higher than all." No sooner had Lutufonissa heard this reply than a plan, which she had never thought of before, occurred to her. She replied, "Why should it not be so? It is a matter entirely under your control." "How so?" asked the Begum. The cunning woman replied, "Let the prince give the throne to his son Khasru."

The Begum made no answer. That day neither of them reverted to this topic, but neither of them forgot it. The Begum was not unwilling that her son should ascend the throne in place of her husband. Selim's love for Meheronissa was as much a thorn in the Begum's side as it was in Lutufonissa's. How could Mán Singh's sister like to obey an upstart Turcoman girl? Lutufonissa, too, had a deep meaning in effecting this resolve. On a subsequent occasion they reverted to this topic, and both made up their minds.

Lutufonissa made the Begum see that there was nothing strange in placing Khasru on Akber's throne to the exclusion of Selim. She said, "The Mogul Empire has been established by the strong arm of the Rajputs. Mán Singh is the ornament of that Rajput race, and he is Khasru's uncle. Again, the chief of the Mussulmans is Khan Azim; he is the principal Minister, and he is Khasru's father-in-law. If they both give their aid, who will not follow them? By whose strength can the prince seize the throne? To get Mán Singh to help us in this matter will be your business; I will see that Khan Azim and other Mohammedan nobles join the conspiracy. With your blessing I shall be successful, but I have one anxiety, lest Khasru, on coming to the throne, may banish this wretched one from the palace."

The Begum understood her companion's wish. She laughed and said, "You can marry any noble in Agra you please, and I will make your husband a mansubdar of five thousand soldiers."

Lutufonissa was satisfied; this was her object. If she must be the wife of some ordinary man in the palace, then wherein lay the pleasure of clipping the wings of the bee that sports on every flower? If she must give up her independence, what pleasure was there in being the slave of the companion of her girlhood, Meheronissa? It was a far more honourable position to be the dearly-loved wife of some chief Minister.

Nor was it solely from this desire that Lutufonissà formed her projects. Selim had neglected her, and was absorbed in Meheronissa. For this she sought revenge.

Khan Azim and the other nobles of Agra and Delhi were to a great extent under Lutufonissa's control. It was not to be wondered at that Khan Azim should aid in accomplishing the wish of his son-in-law. He and other nobles agreed. Khan Azim said to Lutufonissa, "Consider that there is no escape for either of us, if, owing to some mishap, we are successful. Therefore it would be as well to leave some path for saving our lives."

Lutufonissa said, "What do you advise?" Khan Azim said, "There is no refuge except Orissa; it is only in that country that the Mogul Government is not so firm. We must get the Orissa army under our control. Your brother is a mansubdar of Orissa; I will give it out to-morrow that he has been wounded in battle. Do you set out for Orissa to-morrow on the pretence of seeing him? There make all the necessary arrangements, and then return."

Lutufonissa agreed to this proposal. It was while she was on her journey back from Orissa that the reader has been introduced to her.

CHAPTER II.

ON THE WAY.

On the day Moti Bibi or Lutufonissa took leave of Nobokumar and set out for Burdwan, she could not reach Burdwan the same day; she remained in another *chuttee*. At evening she was talking alone with Pesmon, when Moti suddenly asked Pesmon—

"Pesmon, what did you think of my husband?" Pesmon, a little astonished, said, "What should I think of him?" Moti said, "Is he a handsome man or not?"

Pesmon was very angry with Nobokumar. She had been very eager to get the ornaments which Moti had given to Kopal-Kundala, and she had intended one day to ask for them. That hope had now been uprooted; and for this reason she felt a dire resentment against

Kopal-Kundala and her husband. So she replied to the question of her mistress, "What does it signify whether a beggarly Brahman be handsome or ugly?"

Moti understood her companion's thoughts, and said with a laugh, "Suppose the beggarly Brahman becomes a noble, then will he be a handsome man or not?"

Pes. What do you mean?

Moti. Why, don't you know that the Begum has promised that, if Khasru be made king, my husband is to be a noble?

Pes. That I know, but why should your former husband be noble?

Moti. What other husband have I?

Pes. He who will be.

Moti said with a smile, "Two husbands for a chaste woman like me, that is very wrong. Who is that over there?"

Pesmon knew the man pointed out by Moti. He was a resident of Agra, and one of Khan Azim's followers. Both got anxious. Pesmon called him, and the man came, and, making an obeisance to Lutufonissa, put a letter in her hand, and said, "I was taking the letter to Orissa; it is of the utmost importance." On reading the letter, all Moti Bibi's hopes and aspirations disappeared. The purport of the letter was as follows:—

"Our efforts have been unsuccessful. Even on his death-bed Akber Shah has defeated us by the strength of his intellect. His death has taken place, and by his orders, the Prince Selim has now become Jahangir Shah. Do not be anxious on Khasru's account. Quickly return to Agra to guard against any one doing you an injury."

How Akber Shah defeated this conspiracy is written in history; it is not necessary to relate it in this place.

Moti dismissed the messenger with a present, and read the letter to Pesmon. Pesmon said, "What are you going to do now?"

Moti. There is nothing to be done now.

Pes. (thinking for a moment). What does it matter? You will be in exactly the same position as you were before. Every lady in the Mogul Emperor's palace is greater than the queen of any other kingdom.

Moti (smiling). That is no longer possible; I cannot remain any longer in the royal palace. Meheronissa will very soon be married to Jahangir. I know Meheronissa well from a child; when she once gets in the palace, she will become emperor; Jahangir will be emperor in name only. She must know that I attempted to bar her path to the throne. What, then, will happen to me?

Pesmon, almost crying, said, "What are you going to do then?"

Moti said, "There is one hope. How does Meheronissa feel towards Jahangir? Considering how firm she is, if she is not in love with Jahangir, but is really fond of her husband, Jahangir will never win her, not if he kills a hundred Sher Afghans. But if Meheronissa is really enamoured of Jahangir, then there is no further hope.

Pes. How will you find out Meheronissa's feelings?

Moti laughed and said, "What is impossible

to Lutufonissa? Meheronissa is the friend of my childhood; I will go to Burdwan to-morrow, and remain two days with her."

Pes. If Meheronissa loves the king, what will you do?

Moti. My father is in the habit of saying, "In the field action is decided upon."

Both remained silent for a moment. Moti's lips curled with a slight smile. Pesmon asked, "Why are you laughing?"

Moti said, "A new idea has entered my head."

Pesmon asked what it was, but Moti did not tell her. Neither shall we inform the reader. It will become known hereafter.

CHAPTER III.

IN THE RIVAL'S HOUSE.

AT that time Sher Afghan was living as Governor of Burdwan under the Subadar of Bengal.

Moti Bibi came to Burdwan and put up in Sher Afghan's house, where she was treated with much honour by Sher Afghan and his family. Moti Bibi had been well known to Sher Afghan and his wife when they used to live in Agra; and she was a great friend of Meheronissa's. Afterwards they both became rivals for the empire of Delhi. Now that they had come together, Meheronissa thought, "In whose destiny has the Creator written the sovereignty of India? The Creator Himself knows, and Selim knows; and if any one else knows, it is this Lutufonissa. Let me see if she will not reveal something." Moti Bibi, too, wanted to find out Meheronissa's thoughts.

At that time Meheronissa had acquired the reputation of being the most beautiful and virtuous woman in India; and, as a matter of fact, women like her are seldom born in the world. Of those women who are famous in history for their beauty all historians admit her superiority. Very few men of that period excelled her in any branch of knowledge. Meheronissa was unrivalled in song and dance; she fascinated the minds of all by her poems and paintings, and her sparkling conversation was even more charming than her beauty. Nor was Moti deficient in these qualities. To-day these two remarkable women were eager to find out one another's thoughts.

Meheronissa was seated in her private room painting a picture. Moti was sitting just behind her looking on, and was chewing pán. Meheronissa asked, "What do you think of the picture?" Moti Bihi replied, "It is like your paintings always are; it is a pity that now-a-days there is no skilled painter like you."

Mehe. Even if there be not, where is the pity?

Moti. If any other were as skilled as you, they might preserve a model of this face of yours.

Mehe. Will a likeness of the face remain in the earth of the grave?

Meheronissa said this somewhat gravely.

Moti. Sister ——, why so serious to-day?

Mehe. How am I serious? But I cannot forget that you are going to leave me to-morrow morning. Can you not please me by stopping two days more?

Moti. Who does not wish for pleasure? If it were possible to stay, why should I go? But I am the servant of another; how can I remain?

Mehe. You do not love me any more; if you wanted to stay, you could manage it in some way. You have come here, and why can't you remain?

Moti. I have told you all. My brother is a mansubdar in the Mogul army—he was wounded in fight with the Orissa Pathans, and was in much danger. When I heard it, I got leave from the Begum and went to see him. I have stayed too long in Orissa, and ought not to delay any more. I had not seen you for a long time, and for this reason I have remained two days with you.

Mehe. By what day have you agreed to return to the Begum?

Moti understood that Meheronissa was jesting. Moti was not so expert as Meheronissa in neat and biting jests; but neither was she a woman to lose her wits. She replied, "Was it likely that, going on a three months' journey, I should fix any particular day for my return? But I have delayed too long; and further delay may be a cause for displeasure."

Meheronissa said, with one of her world-enchanting smiles, "Whose displeasure do you fear — the prince's, or that of his queen?"

Moti was a little confused, and said, "Why do you wish to put to shame this shameless one? Perhaps the displeasure of both."

Mehe. But let me ask you, Why do you not take the name of Begum yourself? I heard that the Prince Selim was going to marry you and make you the principal Begum. How far is that true?

Moti. I am naturally subject to others; why should I destroy the little independence I have. As the Begum's companion, I have found no difficulty in coming to Orissa; but as Selim's Begum, could I have done so?

Mehe. What necessity could there be for the Emperor of Delhi's chief queen to come to Orissa?

Moti. I have never aspired to be Selim's chief queen. In this country of Hindostan none but Meheronissa is fit to be the loved consort of the Emperor of Delhi.

Meheronissa bent down her head. She remained silent for a moment, and said, "Sister, I do not suppose that you have said this to pain me, or to find out my heart. But I entreat you not to say anything in forgetfulness of the fact that I am Sher Afghan's wife, and, heart and soul, his slave."

The shameless Moti was not confounded by this reproach, which indeed gave her an opportunity for further probing. She said, "I know well that you are devoted to your husband; and for this reason I ventured to introduce this topic by a side-wind. It was my object to let you know that Selim has not yet been able to forget your beauty. Be careful."

Mehe. Now I understand; but what should I fear?

Moti, with some hesitation, said, "Fear of widowhood," and as she spoke she fixed a piercing glance on Meheronissa's face; but she could not perceive any sign of either fear or joy. Meheronissa proudly said, "Fear of widowhood! Sher Afghan is able to defend himself; moreover, in Akber Shah's kingdom even his son cannot take the life of an innocent man with impunity."

Moti. That is true, but the latest news from Agra is that Akber Shah is dead. Selim has ascended the throne. Who will curb Delhi's emperor?

Meheronissa heard no more; her whole body shook and trembled. Again she bent her head, and tears flowed from her eyes. Moti asked, "Why do you cry?"

Meheronissa said with a sigh, "Selim is on the throne of India; where am I?"

Moti's object was achieved; she said, "Can you not even now altogether forget the prince?"

Meheronissa said in a sobbing voice, "Whom shall I forget? I may forget my own life, but I can never forget the prince? But listen, sister! The door of my heart has suddenly opened; you have heard this; but I solemnly adjure you not to tell another."

Moti said, "Well, be it so; but when Selim hears I have been to Burdwan, he will certainly ask me what Meheronissa said of him. What shall I tell him?"

Meheronissa thought for a few moments and said, "Tell him this, that Meheronissa idolises him in her heart, and will lay down her life for him, should necessity arise. But she will never yield her honour, and, as long as her husband lives, she will never look on the face of Delhi's emperor. And if her husband be killed by Delhi's emperor, then in this world she will never meet her husband's murderer."

With these words Meheronissa got up and went away. Moti Bibi was astounded. But the victory was hers; she had found out Meheronissa's feelings, while Meheronissa knew nothing of Moti Bibi's wishes and aspirations. She who afterwards, by the force of her intellect, became the queen of the king of Delhi,—even she was vanquished by Moti. The reason was that Meheronissa was in love, while in this matter Moti Bibi was actuated only by selfish motives.

Moti Bibi knew well the varied movements of man's heart. What she concluded on a consideration of Meheronissa's words, that actually came to pass. She saw that Meheronissa was really in love with Jahangir; therefore, whatever she might say now with a woman's pride, she would never be able to control her feelings, when the path lay open; she would without doubt fulfil the wish of the king.

With this certainty Moti's hopes and aspirations were dashed to the ground; but was Moti grieved on that account? She was not; nay more, she even experienced a certain pleasure. Why she felt so strange a joy, Moti could not at first understand. She set out for Agra. Some days passed on the way, and during that time she understood the feelings of her heart.

CHAPTER IV.

IN THE HOUSE OF THE KING.

MOTI arrived at Agra. It is no longer necessary to call her Moti. In a few days her heart had undergone an entire change.

She saw Jahangir, who received her with the same respect as before, and asked after her brother, and how she had fared on the way. What Lutufonissa said to Meheronissa was true. After some talk on other matters, Jahangir, on hearing Burdwan mentioned, asked, "You were two days with Meheronissa; what did she say about me?" Lutufonissa frankly informed him of Meheronissa's love. The King, hearing it, remained silent; a tear or two dropped from his large eyes.

Lutufonissa said, "Refuge of the world!

your slave has given you good news; hitherto you have ordered no reward for me."

The King laughed and said, "Lady, your desires are boundless."

Lu. Refuge of the world, what is my fault?

King. I have made the king of Delhi your servant. Do you desire any further reward?

Lutufonissa laughed and said, "Women have many desires."

King. What is your last wish?

Lu. First, let it be ordered that your slave's request will be granted.

King. If it will not harm the kingdom in any way.

Lu. (laughing.) The Emperor of Delhi's affairs cannot be harmed for the sake of me.

King. Then I agree; what is your wish? let me hear.

Lu. I want to marry.

Jahangir broke into a loud laugh: "Truly, this is a new wish; and have you decided on a bridegroom?"

Lu. Yes; it only awaits the king's order.

There can be no proper betrothal without the king's order.

King. What is the necessity for my consent ? Whom do you intend to float in this sea of happiness ?

Lu. Your slave is not an adulteress because she has served the king of Delhi. Your slave asks permission to marry her own husband.

King. Indeed! Then what is to become of this old servant ?

Lu. I will give him Meheronissa, empress of Delhi.

King. Who is Meheronissa, empress of Delhi ?

Lu. She who will be.

Jahangir thought that Lutufonissa knew for certain that Meheronissa would become empress of Delhi, and therefore she wanted to leave the royal harem through vexation at the defeat of her own desires. Thinking this, Jahangir was pained, and remained silent. Lutufonissa said, "What! does not the king agree to this betrothal ?"

King. I am not unwilling; but what is the necessity of being married again to your husband?

Lu. Through ill fortune my first husband did not receive me as his wife. Now he will not be able to abandon the slave of the refuge of the world.

The king laughed merrily, and then became grave. He said, "Dear one! I cannot refuse you anything. If you are so inclined, do so. But why should you abandon me? Do not the moon and sun both shine in the same sky? Do not two flowers bloom on the same stalk?"

Lutufonissa fixed her large eyes on the king, and said, "Small flowers may bloom, but there cannot be two lotuses on the same stalk. Why should I remain as a thorn beneath your jewelled throne?"

Lutufonissa went away to her house. She did not divulge to Jahangir the reason for her new desire. Jahangir thought what it was natural to infer, and gave the matter no further thought. He knew nothing of the secret meaning. Lutufonissa's heart was made of stone. Even Selim's princely beauty, that conquered all women, had not charmed her. But this time the worm had entered the stone.

CHAPTER V.

AT HOME.

Lutufonissa came to her house, and calling Pesmon with a cheerful face, took off her jewels and ornaments. She took off her clothes, embroidered with gold, pearls, and other precious stones, and said to Pesmon, "Do you take these clothes."

Pesmon, on hearing this, was a little astonished, as the clothes had quite lately been made at an enormous expense. She said, "Why do you give me the clothes? What is the news to-day?"

Lutufonissa said, "It is good news."

Pe. That I can understand. Have you got rid of the obstacle Meheronissa?

Lu. Yes. Now I have no anxiety on that score.

Pesmon evinced great joy, and said, "Then I am now the servant of the Begum."

Lu. If you wish to be the Begum's servant, I will tell Meheronissa.

Pe. What! you say there is no probability of Meheronissa becoming the king's Begum?

Lu. I did not say so; I said I had no anxiety on that score.

Pe. Why no anxiety? If you are not the sole queen in Delhi, then all is in vain.

Lu. I will have no connection with Agra.

Pe. What! I cannot understand. Then what is this good news? please explain.

Lu. The good news is this, that I am leaving Agra for ever.

Pe. Where are you going?

Lu. I will go and live in Bengal. If possible, I will become some gentleman's wife.

Pe. This is a new jest; but it makes me shudder to hear it.

Lu. I am not jesting. I am really leaving Agra. I have already taken leave of the king.

Pe. Why have you formed this evil resolution?

Lu. It is not an evil resolution. I have been about Agra for a long time, and with what result? My desire for pleasure has always been strong from my childhood. It was to satisfy that thirst that I left Bengal and came here. To purchase this jewel what wealth have I not given? What evil actions have I not committed? And the objects for which I have done all this,—which of them have I not attained? I have drunk to the dregs the cup of riches, prosperity, wealth, grandeur, and fame. And what have I got by all this? To-day, sitting here and counting over the days in my mind, I can say that I have not been happy for a single day; not for a single instant have I experienced any enjoyment. I have never been satisfied: my thirst only increases. If I try, I can acquire more wealth and more riches, but for what? If there were happiness in all this, then in so many days I should have been happy for one day at least. This desire for pleasure is like a mountain-stream,—first a thin, clear stream, issuing from a solitary spot, it conceals itself in its own womb, no one knows it; of itself it makes a trickling sound, and no one hears it. Gradually, as it flows, its body increases, and it becomes more muddy; and not only that,—then again the wind blows, waves are formed, and crocodiles and alligators live in it. Its size increases further, the water becomes still muddier, it gets brackish; sandy barren islands appear on its bosom, the current becomes gradually slower; then where does that muddy river conceal itself? Who can say?

Pe. I cannot make anything out of that. Why do you not take pleasure in all this?

Lu. I have at last understood the reason. On my way back from Orissa I felt on one night that pleasure which I have not felt by sitting three years in the shade of the royal favour. That has made me understand.

Pe. Understand what?

Lu. All this time I have been like a Hindu idol, adorned with gold and jewels outside, but inside stone. I have wandered about in the fire in search of sensual pleasure, but I have never touched the fire. Now let me see if by searching I can find in the stone a heart of blood and veins.

Pe. I cannot understand anything of this either.

Lu. In this Agra have I ever loved anybody?

Pe. (softly.) Not a single one.

Lu. Then if I am not made of stone, what am I?

Pe. Then if you want to love now, why don't you do so?

Lu. I do want to; and that is the reason I am leaving Agra.

Pe. What is the necessity of that? Are there no people in Agra, that you should go to a country of barbarians? Why do you not love him who loves you? whether in beauty, riches, wealth, or aught else, who is greater than the King of Delhi?

Lu. When the sun and moon remain in the sky, why does water fall?

Pe. Why?

Lu. It is the decree of fate.

Lutufonissa did not tell her everything outright. Fire had entered the stone; the stone was being melted.

CHAPTER VI.

AT HIS FEET.

A SEED sown in a field germinates without any extraneous aid. When it becomes a germ, no one knows and no one sees. But, when once the seed is sown, wherever the sower may be, it gradually grows from a germ to a tree, and raises its head aloft. To-day the tree is only the size of a finger, and can just be seen; gradually and imperceptibly it grows; first it is half a cubit high, then a cubit, then two cubits; still, it can scarcely be observed, except by one who has some particular object in doing so. A day, a month, a year, rolls by, gradually the eye falls upon it; it is no longer a thing that can be disregarded; gradually the tree becomes large, and its shade destroys other trees—in short, the field becomes one huge tree.

In such a way had Lutufonissa's love grown. At first, when one day she suddenly met the object of her love, she did not particularly notice any feeling of love; but it was then that the seed germinated. After that there was no further meeting, but again and again she thought of that absent face, and experienced a certain pleasure in painting it on the canvas of her memory. The seed had sprouted; love for the object had sprung up. The peculiarity of the heart is this, that the more some mental work is mastered, the greater is the liking for such work. Lutufonissa every moment thought of that form, and a fierce desire to see it sprung up within her; at the same time the stream of her natural affection became uncontrollable. Even her desire for the throne of Delhi seemed a matter of no moment to her. The throne appeared to her to be surrounded by heaps of fire caused by the arrows of Cupid. Kingdom, capital, throne—she abandoned all, and hastened to look on her darling. That darling was Nobokumar.

For these reasons Lutufonissa was not unhappy on hearing the words of Meheronissa that destroyed her hopes; for these reasons, on coming to Agra, she made no attempt to preserve her property; for these reasons she took leave of the king for ever.

Lutufonissa came to Septogram, and took up her abode in a large house near the high road, in the middle of the city. Those who passed saw that the house had been suddenly filled with male and female slaves, adorned with gold-embroidered clothes. The decoration of the various rooms was very charming. Fragrant perfumes, scents, and flowers shed joy on every side; articles of various sorts, inlaid with gold, silver, and ivory, sparkled everywhere for the adornment of the house. In one of these decorated rooms Lutufonissa was seated with her face bent downwards; on a separate seat was Nobokumar. Lutufonissa had already seen Nobokumar once or twice in Septogram, and how far her desire had been fulfilled thereby will be seen from to-day's conversation.

Nobokumar was silent for a moment, and said, "Then I am off now. Do not send for me again."

Lutufonissa said, "Don't go; wait a little longer: I have not finished what I had to say."

Nobokumar waited another moment or two, but Lutufonissa said nothing. After a little Nobokumar asked, "What else do you want to say?" Lutufonissa made no reply—she was silently weeping.

Nobokumar seeing this, got up. Lutufonissa seized his cloth. Nobokumar said in a tone of slight vexation, "Why don't you speak?"

Lutufonissa said, "What do you want? Is there nothing you desire in the whole world? Wealth, prosperity, honour, love, pleasure, sport,—all that the world calls happiness I will give you. I ask for nothing in return; I only desire to be your slave; to be your wife, I ask not for such greatness,—only your slave!"

Nobokumar said, "I am a poor Brahman, and shall be nothing else in this birth. I cannot take your money and goods and become a Mussulmani's paramour."

A Mussulmani's paramour! Nobokumar had not yet found out that this woman was his wife. Lutufonissa remained with her head bent down. Nobokumar loosed his cloth from her grasp, but she again seized it. "Well, let that pass. If such is the will of God, I will drown my desires in bottomless waters. I wish nothing else but that you should now and again come this way; look on me as your slave, and now and again show yourself,—I will only satisfy my eyes."

Nob. You are a Mussulman—another's wife—there is sin even in such acquaintance with you. I shall never see you again. There was silence for a moment; a storm was raging in Lutufonissa's heart; she remained motionless as a stone image. She let go Nobokumar's cloth, and said, "Go."

Nobokumar moved to go. He had not gone a step or two, when suddenly, like a tree uprooted by the wind, Lutufonissa fell at his feet. She clung round his legs with the creepers of her arms, and said in piteous tones—

"Merciless one! For you I have given up the throne of Agra. Do not forsake me!"

Nobokumar said, "Return to Agra, and give up all hopes of me."

"Never in this life!" Lutufonissa stood up like an arrow and proudly said, "In this life I will never give you up!" Raising her head, and slightly curving her neck, the enchantress of kings stood with her large eyes fixed on Nobokumar. Again flashed forth the light of that ancient divine pride which had melted away in the fire of her heart—that invincible mental power which had not shrunk from the task of ruling the empire of India,—that power again arose in her body, shattered with love. The veins in her forehead swelled, and showed beautiful lines; her lustrous eyes began to flash like the ocean waters sounding in the rays of the sun; her nostrils quivered; as the swan, sporting on the stream, floats with neck curved against the opposing current, as the trodden snake lifts its crest, so stood the mad Mussulman girl, raising her head. She said, "Not in this life. You will be mine, and mine only."

Looking on the form of that angry snake, Nobokumar was frightened. He had never seen Lutufonissa's unspeakable charms as he now saw them. But that beauty was enchanting like the lightning that precedes the thunder-bolt; seeing it he feared. Nobokumar was moving away, when suddenly he remembered another brilliant form. One day Nobokumar, vexed with his first wife, Podmaboti, had been about to drive her out of the sleeping chamber. The girl of twelve years had then proudly turned on him and stood upright; even so had her eyes lighted up; just so had the lines stood out on her forehead; just so had her nostrils quivered; just so had her head shaken. For a long time he had not remembered that form, now he remembered it,—he at once perceived the likeness. Torn with doubts, and in a trembling voice, he softly said, "Who are you?"

The Mussulman girl's eyes grew larger still as she replied, " I am Podmaboti."

Not waiting for a reply, Lutufonissa went away; and Nobokumar, thoughtful and somewhat terrified, went to his house.

CHAPTER VII.

AT THE END OF THE HAMLET.

Going to another room, Lutufonissa closed the door. For two days she did not come out of it; and during this time she made up her mind what she would do, and determined to carry out her resolve. The sun had set. With Pesmon's aid Lutufonissa was dressing herself;—a wondrous dress! no petticoat, no pyjamas,[1] no shawl; there was no sign of a woman's attire. She looked at her dress in the looking-glass, and said to Pesmon, "Well, Pesmon, could you recognise me?"

Pesmon said, "No one could."

Lu. Then I am off. See that no servant goes with me.

Pesmon was a little alarmed, and said, "If

[1] Pyjamas are loose trousers worn by women in Scinde, the Panjab, and parts of the North-Western Provinces.

you will forgive your servant's fault, I will ask you one thing." Lutufonissa said, "What?" Pesmon said, "What is your object?"

Lutufonissa said, "At present, the eternal separation of Kopal-Kundala and her husband. Afterwards, he will be mine."

Pe. Lady! Consider the matter well; that dense jungle, and night coming on. You are alone.

Lutufonissa made no reply, and left the house. She went towards Nobokumar's house at the extremity of a solitary jungly hamlet of Septogram, and when she got there, night came on. Not far from Nobokumar's house was a dense jungle, which the reader may remember. Coming to the edge of it, she sate down under a tree. For some time she sate and thought over the terrible project in which she was engaged. By chance a before-unthought-of aid presented itself.

From where Lutufonissa sat, she heard an uninterrupted droning sound coming from some human being. She stood up, and looking in all directions, saw that there was a light in the forest. Lutufonissa's courage exceeded a man's, and she went where the light was burning. At first, from the cover of a tree, she saw something very strange. She saw that the light which was burning came from a *Hom*[1] sacrifice, and the noise which she heard was the noise of the recitation of *mantras.* She caught one word in the mantra, and that was a name. Immediately she heard the name, Lutufonissa went and sat by the man who was performing the *Hom* sacrifice.

For the present let her sit there. For a long time the reader has heard nothing of Kopal-Kundala, so that it is necessary to say something about her.

[1] A sacrifice performed by burning *ghi* (clarified butter) in fire, and repeating certain *mantras* or incantations.

END OF THE THIRD PART.

PART IV.

CHAPTER I.

THE DEVELOPMENT OF THE PLOT.

To such a pitch of interest has our story arrived. The painter, who paints a portrait, first makes separate outlines of the legs and other members, and finally connects them together and distinguishes the light from the shade. We have up to this point delineated the limbs and members of this mental picture; now we shall join them together and unite the light and shade.

A cloud is produced by the water-vapour drawn up by the sun. Day by day the array of clouds imperceptibly increases. But no one at first marks the cloud, or thinks of it, until at last it entirely darkens the world, and hurls forth a thunder-bolt. The cloud in which Kopal-Kundala's life was suddenly immersed,—up till now we have bit by bit been collecting its vapour and water.

Does the reader believe in destiny? I do not speak of absolute fatalism, which is mere nonsense made up to console the minds of idle men; but does he admit this, that sometimes some coming event in this way casts its shadow before it, and that actions indicating its accomplishment are brought about with so irresistible a force that human power cannot check them? Wise men in all countries and in all ages have admitted this. This destiny is the soul of the "Waverley Novels;" it is the essence of omniscient Shakespeare's "Macbeth." In another form, as "Fate" and "Necessity," it has been the cause of considerable diversity of opinion among European philosophers.

In our own country this "Destiny" is well known in society. The poet, who imagined the destruction of the race of Kurus, was exceedingly skilled in this fascinating spell.

This terrible shadow was ever present over the heads of the Kurus ever since the time when they sported as children with the Pandus. The great Krishna is its best personification. The poet himself has illustrated it in the lamentations of Dhritarashtra and other matters. The holy songs of Bhagbut are full of this destiny. At the present time many, who have read a portion of this poetry, worship destiny. Others, muttering "Kopâl," are ever careless.

I do not mean by destiny that, by some divine or internal power, our actions assume a certain shape. Even atheists may admit destiny. Worldly events are the inevitable outcome of natural laws and man's character; man's character is the result of mental and natural laws. Therefore destiny is the result of mental and natural laws; but those rules are called destiny, because they are beyond man's comprehension.

Some readers may be vexed at the termination of this book. They may say, "The ending is not a good one; the novelist might have made it different." To this my reply is, "It is the course of destiny; who can alter destiny? The novelist cannot do so. As the seed sown at the commencement of the book, so must the product be. To do otherwise would be a blow against truth."

Now let us follow the course of destiny. The threads are ready; let us gather them together.

CHAPTER II.

IN THE SLEEPING-CHAMBER.

About a year had passed since Lutufonissa had reached Agra, and come from there to Septogram. Kopal-Kundala had for more than a year been Nobokumar's wife. The day Lutufonissa went to the jungle at evening, Kopal-Kundala was seated absently in her bed-chamber. She is not the same Kopal-Kundala that the reader has seen on the sea-shore, with her tresses tossed about, and limbs devoid of ornaments. Shamasoondri's prophecy has come true; by the touch of the touchstone the *jogini* has become a *grihini;* now those countless masses of hair, hanging to her ankles, and dazzling black as a swarm of bees, are bound up in a thick knot behind. The arrangement of the knot, too, evinces considerable skill, and a number of fine embroidered threads give evidence of Shamasoondri's skill in doing up hair. Neither have flowers been despised, for they encircle the knot on four sides like a crown. That part of the hair which is not inside the knot, does not lie in one uniform level on the top of the head, but, owing to its curliness, forms a series of small black waves. The face is no longer half-concealed by the mass of hair, but is a blaze of light and beauty, except that here and there a few tiny curls have escaped from their fetters, and moist with perspiration, adhere to the face. Her complexion is beautiful as the rays of the half-moon. Now golden ornaments are swinging from her ears; a golden necklace hangs on her throat. They are not paled by her colour, but are beautiful as a night-flower in the lap of earth, clothed with the light of the half-moon. She has on a white cloth, which is as beautiful as a thin white cloud in a sky lighted by the half-moon.

Though her complexion resembled the

moonlight of the half-moon, still it appeared to be a little paler than before, as when a black cloud is seen in a corner of the sky. Kopal-Kundala was not sitting alone; the fair Shamasoondri was seated near her. They were talking together, and the reader must hear a portion of what they were saying.

Kopal-Kundala said, "How much longer will the son-in-law stay here?"

Shamasoondri said, "He is going to-morrow afternoon. Alas! if I could this night pluck the magic herb, I could bring him under my control, and so render my birth successful. I was cuffed and beaten with a broom yesterday because I went out, so how can I go out to-day?"

K. Why won't it do to pluck it in the daytime?

Sha. If you pluck it by day, why should it flower? It must be plucked with dishevelled hair, exactly at midnight. For this reason, brother,[1] I must bury my wish in my heart.

[1] Brother is a term of endearment used by a girl to a friend.

K. Very well; to-day I recognised that plant, and I know the jungle in which it grows. You will not have to go to-day; I will go alone and bring the drug.

Sha. What has happened is past. Don't go out any more at night.

K. Why are you anxious on that account? You have heard that it has been my practice from a child to roam about at night. Just consider that, if such had not been my practice, I should never have seen you.

Sha. It was not from that fear I spoke; but is it proper for respectable young girls[1] to wander about in the forest at night? I was severely blamed, even when we went together; and if you go alone, you will get into a terrible row.

K. Where's the harm? Do you, too, think that I shall become a bad character, because I go out of the house at night?

Sha. I don't think that; but evil people will say evil things.

K. Let them; that doesn't make me bad.

[1] Literally, respectable daughters-in-law and daughters.

Sha. Quite true. But if any one reproaches you, it will vex us.

K. Don't allow yourself to be vexed for so foolish a reason.

Sha. That I shouldn't; but why should you pain my brother?

K. Kopal-Kundala cast on Shamasoondri one of her bright affectionate glances, and said: "If he is pained by this, what am I to do? Had I known that marriage for a woman means slavery, I should never have married!"

After that Shamasoondri thought it better to say nothing further. She got up and went to her work.

Kopul-Kundala busied herself with the necessary household duties, and having completed them, she went out of the house in search of the medicine. Then it was more than one *pahar* of the night. The night was moonlight. Nobokumar was seated in the outer room, and saw from the window that Kopal-Kundala was going out. He, too, went out and seized Mrinomoi by the arm. Kopal-Kundala said, "What is it?"

Nobokumar said, "Where are you going?"

There was no sound of rebuke in his voice.

Kopal-Kundala said, "Shamasoondri wants a drug for bringing her husband under her control, and I am going out to look for it."

Nobokumar said as tenderly as before, "Very well, you went once yesterday! Why again to-day?"

K. Yesterday I could not find it; I will look for it again.

Nobokumar said very mildly, "Wouldn't it do as well to look for it in the day-time?" Nobokumar's voice was full of love. Kopal-Kundala said, "The drug does not flower by day."

Mot. What is the use of your looking for the medicine? Tell me the name of the plant, and I will pluck and bring it for you.

K. I know the tree, if I see it; but I don't know its name. And it won't do for you to pluck it. A woman must pluck it with her hair all loose. Do not put any obstacle in the way of another's benefit.

Kopal-Kundala said this with some harshness. Nobokumar made no further objection. He said, "Come, I will go with you."

Kopal-Kundala said proudly, "Come; see with your own eyes if I am unworthy of confidence or not."

Nobokumar could say nothing further. With a sigh he let go Kopal-Kundala's hand, and returned to his house. Kopal-Kundala alone entered the forest.

CHAPTER III.

IN THE HEART OF THE FOREST.

It has been to a certain extent mentioned above that this part of Septogram was wooded. Not far from the village was a dense forest. Kopal-Kundala went alone in search of the medicine along a narrow jungle path. The night was soft and perfectly still. In the sky of the spring night the moon with its cool rays was noiselessly passing through the white clouds; on the earth, the forest trees and creepers were as noiselessly resting in the rays of the cold moon; the leaves of the trees were noiselessly reflecting those rays; and noiselessly white flowers shone out midst the creepers and shrubs. The beasts and birds were silent, except that somewhere at intervals could be heard the flapping of the wings of some bird aroused from its rest, and now and again here and there the noise of dry leaves falling; elsewhere, too, might be heard the noise of snakes gliding through the dry leaves on the ground, and ever and anon in the far distance the barking of some dog. Not that the wind was altogether dead; it was the soothing breeze of spring, very gentle, and altogether noiseless, such as to shake only the very topmost leaves of the trees. Only the Shám creeper, bent to the ground, was moving to and fro; only small white clouds were softly moving through the blue sky. Only by the touch of such a breeze was the faint recollection of former happiness awakened in the heart.

Kopal-Kundala's recollection of the past was similarly awakened; she thought of how, on the summits of the sand-hills, the southern breeze laden with drops of ocean-water used to sport amid her long tresses. She gazed at the clear, blue, endless sky, and remembered the ocean so like it. Kopal-Kundala walked along, lost in the recollection of past events.

Absently walking along, Kopal-Kundala did not think of where she was going or with what object. The path gradually became impassable, and the forest more dense; over her head the interwoven branches of trees almost entirely shut out the light of the moon, so that she could no longer perceive the way. This fact first awoke her from her reverie, and, looking here and there, she saw that a light was burning in the forest. Lutu-fonissa, too, had before seen this light. Thanks to her former life, Kopal-Kundala was all this time fearless, but curious. Softly she went in the direction of the light, and saw that no one was there. But not far from it, invisible from a distance owing to the density of the jungle, was a broken house. The house was made of brick, but very small and wretched, and consisted of one room only. The sound of human voices was coming from the house. With noiseless footsteps Kopal-Kundala approached the house, and, no sooner had she got near, than she thought she perceived the sound of two persons engaged in cautious conversation. At first she could not understand a word, but afterwards, when her hearing had been sharpened by close attention, she heard something like the following :—

One was saying, "I desire her death; and if you do not consent to this, I will not help you ; neither do you help me."

The other one said, "Neither do I desire her good; but I agree to her eternal exile only. You will never get me to help you in murdering her; nay, I will oppose such an object."

The first speaker said, "You are very foolish, senseless one! I will teach you some wisdom; listen attentively. I will tell you a great secret; just take a look round once, I thought I heard a man's breathing."

As a matter of fact Kopal-Kundala, in order to hear the conversation well, was standing quite close to the wall of the room; and her eagerness and apprehension combined made her breathe hard and fast.

One of the persons inside the house came out and saw Kopal-Kundala; the latter, too, saw well in the clear moonlight the form of a strange man, and, seeing him, she could not make up her mind whether to be alarmed or glad. She saw that the stranger had on the garb of a Brahman ; that he wore an ordinary *dhotee*, and his body was well covered with a sheet. The Brahman youth was of very tender years, and there was not a single mark of age in his face. His face was very beautiful, beautiful as that of a beautiful woman, but marked with a fire and dignity that a woman's face seldom has. His hair was not cut close like the hair of most men, but uncut like a woman's it lay in masses on his back, limbs, arms, and sometimes on his breast. His forehead was broad, and slightly swollen, a single vein standing out in the middle. His eyes were filled with a lightning lustre. A long naked sword was in his hand. But in the midst of this heap of beauty there was a terrible expression, as if the shadow of some terrible desire had fallen on the golden colour. On seeing a glance that penetrated her inmost heart, Kopal-Kundala felt afraid.

Each looked at the other for an instant.

At first Kopal-Kundala cast down her eyes, and, when she did so, the stranger asked her, "Who are you?"

If a year before, in the thorn jungles of Hidgellee, Kopal-Kundala had been asked this question, she could instantly have given a connected reply; but now Kopal-Kundala had to a certain extent acquired the nature of a family woman,[1] so that she could not at once

[1] It is wrong for a respectable woman to look at or talk to a stranger. Among the higher classes it is of course considered wrong for a woman even to go in a public place unless in a conveyance or palki, or accompanied by other matrons. It has been said that the *zenana* system was the result of the Mohammedan invasion. But probably women were secluded long before that. The word *oborodh* (female apartments) was used before Mohammedan times. Panini gives as an epithet of a king's wife "asuryam-pasya," *i.e.* "one who never sees the sun." In Ramayaná (vi. 99–33) there is clear allusion to some sort of seclusion being practised. Rama thinks it necessary to excuse himself for permitting his wife to expose herself to the gaze of the crowd.

Chivalry and reverence for the fair sex belonged only to European nations of northern origin, who were the first to hold that "inesse fœminis sanctum aliquid" (Tac. Germ. 8). Yet it is clear from many passages that women had more liberty than now. Rama says to Vihishana:—"In great calamities, at marriages, at the public choice of a husband by maidens, at a sacrifice, at assemblies, it is allowable for all the world to look upon women." Sakuntala appears in the public court of King Dushyanta; Damayanti travels about by her-make any reply. The man in Brahman garb, seeing Kopal-Kundala did not reply, said, "Kopal-Kundala, why have you come at night into this dense forest?"

Hearing her name from an unknown night-prowler, Kopal-Kundala was speechless, and a little terrified, so that a reply did not readily come from her mouth.

The man in Brahman garb again asked, "Did you hear my question?"

Suddenly Kopal-Kundala regained her power of speech. Without replying, she said, "I too must ask that question. What evil conspiracy are you two concocting by night in this forest?"

The man in Brahman garb remained for some time silent and immersed in thought, as if some new means of accomplishing his purpose had entered into his mind. He took Kopal-Kundala by the hand, and led her

self; the mother of Rama goes to the hermitage of Valmiki. Again, women were present at dramatic representations, rode on horses, visited the temples of the gods, and performed their ablutions with little or no privacy, which is still the custom, though not among well-to-do Mohammedan women.

some distance from the broken house. Kopal-Kundala in great wrath released her hand. The man in Brahman garb said very softly, close to Kopal-Kundala's ear, "What do you fear? I am not a man."

Kopal-Kundala was more astounded. She was inclined to believe it, but did not entirely do so. She went with the woman clad as a Brahman. Coming to a secret place away from the house, the Brahman whispered to Kopal-Kundala, "Will you hear what we were conspiring? It concerns you."

Kopal-Kundala's fear and curiosity increased; she said, "I will hear it."

The disguised woman said, "Then wait here till my return." And with this word she returned to the broken house. Kopal-Kundala remained sitting there for some time. But she was exceedingly alarmed by what she had seen and heard; and, sitting alone in the dark forest, her fear increased, especially as it was impossible to say with what object the disguised one had seated her there. It might be that he had placed her there in order to accomplish his evil purpose. Thinking this, Kopal-Kundala was overwhelmed with fear. The Brahman was a long time in returning, and Kopal-Kundala could sit no longer. She got up and ran quickly in the direction of her house.

Then the sky began to grow black with clouds; even the little light there was in the forest began to disappear. Kopal-Kundala could not delay another moment. She quickly began to come out from the midst of the forest, and as she came, she fancied she could hear the footsteps of some one behind her; but, turning round, she could see nothing in the darkness. Kopal-Kundala thought the Brahman was pursuing her. She left the jungle and came out on the small forest-path mentioned above. There it was not so dark; a man could be seen, but she saw nothing. Therefore she went on her way quickly; but again she plainly heard footsteps. The sky became more terrible with black clouds. Kopal-Kundala ran faster. Not far from her house, but before she had actually reached it, a terrible storm of rain came down with a terrific noise. Kopal-Kundala ran, and she fancied the man behind her was also running. Before she could see her house, the wind and rain came down on Kopal-Kundala's house. There were claps of thunder in quick succession, and the noise of the falling of thunderbolts. The lightning flashed incessantly, while the rain fell in sheets. Kopal-Kundala somehow managed to escape into the house. She crossed the yard, and entered her room. The door was open for her. She turned facing the yard in order to close the door, and as she did so she fancied she saw a tall man standing in the yard. At that moment there was a single flash of lightning, and in that single flash she recognised him. It was the Kapálik who dwelt by the sea-shore.

CHAPTER IV.

IN A DREAM.

KOPAL - KUNDALA quietly shut the door. Quietly she came to her bed-chamber, and quietly she lay down on her bed. Man's heart is an endless sea; when the winds rush and battle over it, who can count its waves? Who could count the waves surging up in the sea of Kopal-Kundala's heart?

That night Nobokumar's heart was pained, and he did not come to the female apartments. Kopal-Kundala lay alone in her bed-chamber, but she did not sleep. Even in the darkness she saw everywhere that face encircled with matted hair, blown by the strong winds, and moist with streams of water. Kopal-Kundala began to think of the past events of her life; she remembered the way in which she had left the Kapálik; she remembered the devilish rites the Kapálik used to perform in the dense forest; the worship of Bhoirobi performed by him; the imprisonment of Nobokumar—all this she thought of. Kopal-Kundala shuddered. She thought too of the events of that night—Shama's desire for the medicine, Nobokumar's prohibition, her rebuking him, then the moonlight beauty of the forest, the darkness in the midst of it, the splendid and terrible beauty of the companion she had found in the forest—all came before her.

The east was marked with the crowning light of dawn. Then Kopal-Kundala got a little sleep, but a light restless sleep, in which she had dreams. It seemed to her that she was going along in a boat on the bosom of the ocean she had seen before. The boat was beautifully adorned, and a green flag was flying from it; the oarsmen were rowing with garlands of flowers on their necks, and singing the endless loves of Radha and Sham. From the western sky the sun was raining streams of gold; the sea, receiving them, was laughing; in the sky the clouds were running to and fro, and bathing themselves in that golden shower. Suddenly it became night, and the sun disappeared. The golden clouds, too, disappeared, and a dense black cloud came and overspread the sky. The direction could no longer be ascertained. The oarsmen turned the boat, and were uncertain in what direction to row. They stopped her, and tore the garlands from their necks; the green flag slipped down and fell into the water. The wind arose; waves as large as trees began to rise; from the midst of a wave a man of terrible appearance, wearing matted hair, came, and, lifting up Kopal-Kundala's boat with his left hand, was about to send it to the bottom, when that terribly beautiful one, dressed as a Brahman, came and seized the boat, and said to Kopal-Kundala, "Shall I preserve you or drown you?" Suddenly the words "Drown me" issued from Kopal-Kundala's mouth. The Brahman let go the boat. Then the boat too was endued with sound, and spoke, and said, "I cannot carry this burden any longer; I will enter hell." So saying the boat flung her into the waters and entered hell.

Kopal-Kundala woke from her dream, covered with heavy perspiration, and opened her eyes. She saw that it was morning. The window of the room was open, and the current of the spring breeze was blowing through it; the birds were singing on the branches of the trees, softly swaying to and fro; over the window some charming jungle-creepers were swinging with their fragrant flowers. Kopal-Kundala, woman as she was, began to pluck the creepers, and, as she was arranging them, a letter dropped out. Kopal-Kundala was an Adhikari's pupil, and could read. She read something like the following:—

"To-day after evening come and meet the young Brahman you saw yesterday night. You shall hear that something of great importance which you wished to hear. This is from the person who wears a Brahman's garb."

CHAPTER V.

IN DOUBT WHAT TO DO.

THAT whole day till evening Kopal-Kundala thought of nothing else but whether it was fitting or not to meet the Brahman. She felt no compunction on the ground of its being improper for a chaste young woman to meet an unknown man at night and alone; as far as that matter was concerned, she was clearly of opinion that, provided the object of the meeting were not wrong, the meeting itself was not wrong. In the same way as a man may meet a man and a woman a woman, so it appeared to her that a woman ought to be able to meet a man. Moreover, it was doubtful whether the Brahman were a man or not. Therefore anxiety on that score was superfluous; but whether good or harm would result from this interview,—it was uncertainty on this score that made Kopal-Kundala hesitate to such an extent. First the conversation of the Brahman, then the sight of the Kapálik, then the dream,—all these reasons made Kopal-Kundala entertain great alarm on her own account; her fear that some harm would soon happen to her had become strong, and she did not consider it altogether improbable that such harm was connected with the arrival of the Kapálik. This Brahman appeared to be his companion—therefore she might fall into disaster by meeting him. He had clearly said that the consultation was about Kopal-Kundala; but it might also be that through him she could get some indication by which she would ascertain this. The young Brahman was taking secret counsel with somebody, and that somebody appeared to be the Kapálik. It was clear, too, that in that conversation somebody's death was being resolved upon, or at any rate eternal banishment. Whose? The Brahman had clearly said that the conspiracy concerned Kopal-Kundala.

Then they were planning her death or her eternal exile. Then, if the Brahman was an abettor in these nefarious schemes, there might be danger in going with him alone at night into a terrible forest. But last night she had seen a dream ; what was the meaning of that dream? In her dream the Brahman, at a time of dire danger, had come and wished to save her; perhaps that was really to happen, and the Brahman wished to tell her all. She had said in the dream, "Drown me;" but should she say that in real life? Should she abandon the Brahman's aid and plunge into the sea of danger? No, no. Bhobani, fond of her devotees, had kindly pointed out in her dream a means of preservation, and the Brahman now wished to deliver her; if she forsook his aid, she would be drowned. For this reason Kopal-Kundala determined to see him. Whether a wise person would have come to this conclusion, is doubtful; but I have no concern with a wise man's resolution. Kopal-Kundala was not particularly wise, therefore she did not resolve like a wise man.

She resolved like a curious woman; like a young woman who was anxious to see a terrible and splendid beauty, like one who had been reared by a Sonyasi,[1] and loved to roam by night in the forests, like one who was stupefied by her intense reverence for Bhobani, like an insect about to fall into the flame of burning fire.

After evening, having finished a portion of the household duties, Kopal-Kundala started for the forest as before. Before going she lighted a light in her bed-chamber. Immediately she left the room the light went out.

On leaving, Kopal-Kundala forgot one thing, namely, where had the Brahman told her to meet him? She must again read the letter. She returned to the house, and looked in the place where she had put the letter that morning, but could not find it. She remembered that, on doing up her hair, she had tied the letter in her top-knot. So she put her

[1] *Sonyasi*, a devotee or ascetic; literally, one who has abandoned all desire for worldly things. The life of a Sonyasi is the fourth stage of existence.

fingers in her hair and searched. Not finding the letter, she loosened her hair; still it was not there. Then she searched in different parts of the house. Not finding it anywhere, she concluded that the former place of meeting must be the place, and again started. For want of time, she could not again do up those abundant tresses of hair; so to-day Kopal-Kundala went her way enveloped in her masses of hair, like the time when she was a virgin.

CHAPTER VI.

AT THE DOOR OF THE HOUSE.

JUST before evening, when Kopal-Kundala was engaged in her household duties, the letter had slipped from her hair and fallen on the ground unperceived by her. Nobokumar had observed it fall from her hair, and was astonished. When Kopal-Kundala had gone elsewhere, he picked up the letter and went outside and read it. There could only be one inference from that letter. "You will hear what you wanted to hear yesterday." What was that? Words of love? Was the Brahman Mrinomoi's paramour? For one who knew the occurrence of the former night, no other conclusion was possible.

When a chaste woman dies with her husband, or when anybody for any other reason ascends the funeral pyre alive, and places the torch to the wood, at first a heap of smoke envelops everything; it shuts out the view; makes all dark; then when the heap of wood gradually begins to burn, at first one or two flames of fire dart from below like serpent's tongues, and lick the limbs here and there, then with a noise the flames of fire come from all sides and spread over every limb and member; at last, with a terrible noise, the heap of fire lights up the sky, leaps over the head, and reduces the body to ashes.

This is what happened to Nobokumar when he read the letter. At first he could not understand it; then doubt, then certainty, and at last agony. Man's heart cannot at once assimilate an excess of pain or an excess of joy; it does so by degrees. At first the heap of smoke enveloped Nobokumar; then the flame of fire began to burn his heart; and at last his heart was reduced to ashes in the heap of fire. Before this Nobokumar had perceived that Kopal-Kundala in some matters did not obey him. Moreover, in spite of his prohibition,

Kopal-Kundala used to go alone wherever she liked; she would behave with anybody as she pleased; and what was more, she would pay no heed to his words, and wander alone in the forest at night. Any one else would have had his suspicions aroused by this, but Nobokumar did not permit himself to doubt for a single moment, knowing that if he once doubted Kopal-Kundala, it would be like the sting of a scorpion, never to be eradicated. To-day, too, he would not have allowed himself to doubt, but to-day it was not a matter of doubt. Certainty had come in its place.

When the first pang of his anguish was over, Nobokumar sate in silence and wept for a long time. He was a little relieved by his tears. Then he made up his mind what to do. To-day he would say nothing to Kopal-Kundala, but, when she started for the forest, he would secretly follow her; he would witness with his own eyes Kopal-Kundala's great sin, and then commit suicide. He would say nothing to Kopal-Kundala, but kill himself. What else could he do? He could no longer bear the terrible burden of life.

With this resolve, he remained watching the back-door to see when Kopal-Kundala would go out. When Kopal-Kundala had gone out a little way, Nobokumar was about to go out too, when Kopal-Kundala returned for the letter. Nobokumar, seeing her, got on one side. At last Kopal-Kundala again went out, and when she had gone some way, Nobokumar was about to follow her, when he saw that a tall man was standing in the doorway.

Who he was, or why he stood there, Nobokumar had no desire to know. He saw him, but took no notice of him; all he wanted was to keep Kopal-Kundala in sight. So, to clear the way, he put his hand on the stranger's breast, and pushed him, but he could not move him.

Nobokumar said, "Who are you? Go—get out of my way."

The stranger said, "Don't you know who I am?"

The sound fell upon his ear like the roaring of the ocean. Nobokumar gazed at him, and saw that it was his old acquaintance, the matted-haired Kapálik!

Nobokumar started, but he was not afraid. Suddenly his face beamed with joy as he asked, "Is Kopal-Kundala going to meet you?" The Kapálik said "No."

The flame of hope, that had flickered for an instant, went out, and Nobokumar's face became cloudy and dark as before. He said, "Then let me pass."

The Kapálik said, "I will let you pass, but I have something to say to you—first hear it."

Nobokumar said, "What should I say to you? Have you again come to take my life? Take it; this time I will offer no resistance. Do you now wait for me, I will return. Why should I not give my body for the satisfaction of the god? I have now reaped its fruits. She who preserved me has now destroyed me. Kapálik! this time do not doubt me; I will this instant return and deliver myself up to you."

The Kapálik said, "I have not come to kill you. That is not Bhobani's wish. What I have come to do will please you. Go inside the house, and listen to what I have to say."

Nobokumar said, "Not now. I will hear it at some other time. Do you wait now. I have some particular business; I will finish it and come."

The Kapálik said, "Child! I know all. You want to follow that wicked woman; I know where she is going. I will take you there with me. I will show you what you want to see; now listen to me, and have no fear."

Nobokumar said, "I no longer fear you. Come."

So saying Nobokumar took the Kapálik inside the house, and gave him a seat, and he, too, sate down and said, "Speak."

CHAPTER VII.

A SECOND MEETING.

THE Kapálik took a seat, and showed his two arms to Nobokumar, who saw that both arms were broken.

The reader may remember that on the night when Nobokumar fled with Kopal-Kundala from the sea-shore, the Kapálik, in his search for them, had fallen from the summit of a sand-hill. He saved his body by holding out his hands, but his two arms were thereby broken. The Kapálik told all this to Nobokumar, and said, "The performance of my rites and ceremonies has not been much hindered by this, but I no longer have any strength in them; it hurts me even to collect wood."

Then he continued, "Not that I knew when I fell that my hands were broken, and my other limbs safe. When I fell I became unconscious. At first I remained in a senseless state; then for a moment I was conscious, and then became senseless again. I cannot say how long I remained in this state; I think it must have been two nights and one day. At morning my consciousness entirely returned, and just before it did so, I had a dream. It seemed to me that Bhobani"—and as he spoke the Kapálik's body quivered—"it seemed as if Bhobani came and appeared to me in person. She frowned and chid me; she was saying, 'O wicked one, the impurity of your heart has caused this hindrance to my worship. You have been a slave to your passions so long, and therefore have not worshipped me with the blood of this virgin. This virgin shall destroy the fruits of your former worship; I will never accept any more worship from you.' Then when I cried and rolled at the mother's feet she was appeased, and said, 'Good man! I will give you but one means of atonement. Offer up that Kopal-Kundala as a sacrifice to me; and until you do so, do not worship me any more!'

"It is not necessary for me to relate after how long or how I recovered. Yesterday I had entirely recovered, and began my endeavour to carry out the order of the goddess. I saw that my two arms had not even the strength of a child. Without a strong arm, my efforts were not likely to be successful. Therefore it became necessary to get a companion. But men are little inclined for religion—by the strength of the iron age[1] a Mussulman is king, and through fear of his wicked rule none was willing to aid me in such a work. After much search I have found out the dwelling of the wicked one; but, through the weakness of my arms, I am unable to obey Bhobani's order. Only for the accomplishment of my will I perform ceremonies according to the rules of the

[1] *Iron Age.* The káli-yuga or fourth age of the world is supposed to commence at the death of Krishna. The Hindu idea of a succession of four yugas or ages, in which a gradual deterioration of the human race takes place, has its counterpart among the Romans in the Golden, Silver, Brazen, and Iron Ages, as described in Ovid's Metamorphoses (I. 89, &c.). The names of the four ages are connected with throws of dice; *krita* being the best throw; *treta,* the next best; *dwapara,* the throw of two; and *kali* being the throw of one only, or the worst throw.

Tantras. Last night I was performing the *Hom* sacrifice in an adjacent jungle, and with my own eyes I saw Kopal-Kundala meet a young Brahman. To-day she is going to meet him. If you want to see, come with me, and I will show you.

"Child! Kopal-Kundala is fit to be sacrificed. At Bhobani's order I will slay her. She too has abused your trust, she should be slain by you too; therefore give me your aid in this. Seize this faithless one, and bring her with me to the place of sacrifice. There sacrifice her with your own hand. By this means the offence, which you have committed against the goddess, will be pardoned; by a holy deed you will gain imperishable virtue, and the faithless one will be punished; there will be an end of vengeance."

The Kapálik finished speaking. Nobokumar made no reply. Seeing his silence, the Kapálik said, "Child! now come and see what I promised to show you."

Nobokumar, with his body bathed in perspiration, went with the Kapálik.

CHAPTER VIII.

THE MEETING OF THE TWO WIVES.

KOPAL-KUNDALA left the house and entered the forest. She first went to the broken house, and there she saw the Brahman. Had it been day she could have seen that his face was very pale. The Brahman said to Kopal-Kundala, "The Kapálik may come here, it is better not to say anything here. Come to another place."

In the forest there was a narrow space surrounded by trees; it was clear in the middle, and a path issued from it. The Brahman took Kopal-Kundala there. When they were both seated, the Brahman said, "First of all, I must make myself known. You can yourself judge how far I am to be believed. When you were returning with your husband from the country of Hidgellee, one night by the way you met a Mussulman girl. Do you remember that?"

Kopal-Kundala said, "The one who gave me the ornaments?"

The Brahman said, "I am she."

Kopal-Kundala was exceedingly startled.

Lutufonissa, seeing her astonishment, said, "There is more to astonish you. I am your co-wife."[1]

Kopal-Kundala, in amazement, said, "What is that?"

Lutufonissa then related the events of her past life in succession; her marriage, the destruction of her caste, her being abandoned by her husband, Dacca, Agra, Jahangir, Meheronissa, her leaving Agra, her living in Septogram, her meeting with Nobokumar, Nobokumar's conduct, her coming in disguise the evening before to the jungle, her meeting with the *Hom* devotee—she told all. At this moment Kopal-Kundala asked, "With what purpose did you wish to come in disguise into our house?"

[1] A first wife calls her husband's second wife her *sotin*.

Lutufonissa said, "In order to separate you and your husband for ever."

Kopal-Kundala began to ponder, and said, "How would you have accomplished that?"

Lutufonissa. For the present I should have caused your husband to doubt your chastity. But there is no necessity to speak of that, as I have abandoned that course. Now if you act according to my advice, my wish will be accomplished through you, and it will be to your benefit.

Kopa. Whose name did you hear in the month of the Homkári?

Lu. Your name. To find out if he was sacrificing for your good or your evil, I made him an obeisance and sate near him. I sate there till his rites were finished. At the end of the sacrifice I asked him the meaning of the sacrifice in which your name occurred. After some talk with him, I came to know that the object of the sacrifice was to injure you. That, too, was my object, and I told him so. There and then we bound ourselves to aid one another, and, in order to take counsel better, he took me into the broken house. Then he told me of his wish, namely, your death. But I did not wish for that. I have committed nothing but evil in this birth, but I have not become so utterly vile as to encompass the death of an innocent girl. I did not agree to it. At that moment you came up. I fancy you must have heard something.

Kopa. I heard some discussion of that sort.

Lu. The man, thinking me senseless and foolish, wished to instruct me. Knowing what would happen at last, and intending to put you on your guard, I took and concealed you in the forest.

Kopa. After that, why did you not return?

Lu. He said much, and a relation of all the details occupied a long time. You know the man well. Can't you guess?

Kopa. My old guardian the Kapálik.

Lu. Yes. The Kapálik told me of everything, first his finding you on the sea-shore, his bringing you up there, Nobokumar's arrival, and your flight with him. What happened after your flight, that too he related. You don't know all that, and I will tell you at length for your information.

Lutufonissa then proceeded to tell of the Kapálik's falling from the hill, the breaking of his arms, and his dream. Hearing of the dream, Kopal-Kundala started and shuddered, and became as restless as lightning. Lutufonissa went on, "The Kapálik's firm resolve is to carry out the behest of Bhobani. As he has lost the strength of his arms, he must have the aid of another. Thinking me to be a Brahman youth, he told me all in the hope of my helping him. Hitherto I have not agreed to this wickedness. I cannot be certain of my evil heart, but I think I should never consent. Nay, it is my intention to oppose this resolve, and it was with this intention that I have come to see you. But I am not altogether disinterested in this matter. I give you your life. You must do something for me."

Kopal-Kundala said, "What shall I do?"

Lu. Give me too my life—abandon your husband.

Kopal-Kuudala for a long time said nothing. After a long silence she said: "If I leave my husband, where am I to go?"

Lu. To a foreign country—far away. I will give you a large house, I will give you wealth, I will give you male and female slaves; you will live like a queen.

Kopal-Kundala again pondered. She saw every part of the world with the eyes of her mind, but nowhere could she see anybody. She gazed into her own heart, she could not see Nobokumar there; then why should she stand in the way of Lutufonissa's pleasure? She said to Lutufonissa—

"I cannot now understand whether you have done me a benefit or not. I have no need of a fine house, wealth, property, male and female slaves. Why should I stand in the way of your happiness? Let your wish be accomplished; from to-morrow you will hear nothing of her who stands in your way. I was a denizen of the forests, and will again become one."

Lutufonissa was astonished, as she had not expected so speedy a consent. She was charmed, and said, "Sister, may you live for ever! You have given me my life. But I will not let you go unprotected. To-morrow morning I will send you a faithful and very intelligent handmaiden of mine. Go with her. In Burdwan a lady of very high rank is my friend; she will satisfy all your wants."

Lutufonissa and Kopal-Kundala were so engaged in their conversation, that they could not at all perceive the obstacle in front of them. They did not see that the Kapálik and Nobokumar were standing at the end of the jungle path, which led out of their place of refuge, and were gazing on them with fierce glances.

Nobokumar and the Kapálik had only observed them, but unfortunately from such a distance they could not hear a single word of their conversation. If man's eyes and ears could go equally far, who can say whether the current of his unhappiness would be decreased or enhanced? People say that the mechanism of the world is wonderfully contrived.

Nobokumar saw that Kopal-Kundala's tresses were hanging loose. When Kopal-Kundala was not his, then she used not to bind up her hair. Again he saw that those tresses, falling on the young Brahman's back, had mingled with his hair that also hung down his limbs. Kopal-Kundala's tresses were so abundant, and they were both seated so close together in order to talk in a low voice, that Kopal-Kundala's hair spread right over Lutufonissa's back. They did not notice this; but Nobokumar, seeing it, gently sank on the ground.

Seeing this, the Kapálik opened a cocoa-nut vessel that hung from his waist, and said, "Child! you are losing your strength, drink this sovereign medicine; it is the gift of Bhobani. By drinking it you will get strength."

The Kapálik held the vessel near Nobokumar's lips. He absently took a draught, and satisfied his burning thirst. Nobokumar did not know that this sweet beverage was exceedingly strong wine prepared by the Kapálik's own hands. Immediately on drinking he regained his strength.

On this side Lutufonissa continued to speak to Kopal-Kundala in a low voice as before.

"Sister! I have no power to recompense you sufficiently for your action; but I shall be happy so long as you always recollect me. I have heard that you bestowed on a poor person the ornaments I gave you. I have now nothing with me. Thinking it might be necessary yesterday, I put a ring in my hair, but by God's favour it was not necessary for that evil purpose. Do you keep this ring. Hereafter, when you look on it, think of your Mussulman sister. To-day, if your husband asks you where you got the ring, say that Lutufonissa gave it to you." With these words, Lutufonissa took from off her finger a ring of great value and put it in Kopal-Kundala's hand. Nobokumar saw this also; the Kapálik had hold of him, and seeing him tremble again, he made him drink another draught of wine. The wine mounted to

Nobokumar's brain, and began to destroy his nature, even uprooting the very seeds of his affection.

Kopal-Kundala took leave of Lutufonissa and went towards her house. Then Nobokumar and the Kapálik, unseen by Lutufonissa, began to follow Kopal-Kundala.

CHAPTER IX.

TOWARDS THE HOUSE.

KOPAL-KUNDALA went slowly towards her house—very slowly and very softly, for she was immersed in deep thought. Lutufonissa's words had completely changed Kopal-Kundala's ideas. She was prepared to sacrifice herself. Self-sacrifice for whom? For Lutufonissa? No.

Kopal-Kundala was at heart a Tantrik's child. As, from a desire for the favour of the goddess Káli, a Tantrik does not shrink from taking another's life, so, from the same desire, Kopal-Kundala was ready to sacrifice her own life. Not that Kopal-Kundala had, like the Kapálik, entirely devoted herself to asking the favour of the goddess; still, by hearing, seeing, and practising devotion towards her day and night, a love for Káli had become rooted in her mind, and she firmly believed that Bhoirobi was the ruler of the universe and the giver of salvation. Her sympathetic heart could not endure that Káli's place of worship should be drenched with human blood, but she was not remiss in showing her devotion in all other matters. Now that Bhoirobi, ruler of the world, she who bestows happiness and pain, giver of future salvation,—she had ordered her in a dream to give up her life. And why should not Kopal-Kundala obey that order?

You and I do not wish to leave life. Whatever we may say in anger, this life is sweet. In expectation of pleasure we wander about in the world like a ball—there is no expectation of pain. If now and again, owing to our own fault, our expectations are not realised, then we loudly cry out about our unhappiness. But for all that, it is certain that pain is not the rule, but only the exception. You and I have happiness everywhere, and it is through such happiness that we are bound to the world, and do not wish to leave it. But in these fetters of the world love is the principal link. Kopal-Kundala had not that link—she had no tie at all. Then who should keep Kopal-Kundala?

He who has no ties, his force is irresistible. Who can stop the torrent that falls from the mountain-top? When once it is driven by the wind, who can stop its spray? When Kopal-Kundala's heart was restless, who was to steady and control it? Who can calm the madness of the young wild elephant?

Kopal-Kundala asked her heart, "Why should I not lay this body at the feet of the ruler of the world? If I die, what then?" She was putting the question, but could not give any certain reply. Even if the world has no other fetter, there is the one fetter of death.

Kopal-Kundala walked on with her head downwards. When man's heart is full of some terrible feeling, and he is so absorbed in thought that he does not notice outward objects, at such a time even unreal things are clearly seen. Such was Kopal-Kundala's state. It appeared to her that a sound entered her ear from above, "Child, I am showing you the way." Kopal-Kundala was startled, and casting her eyes up, saw a form that put to shame the new clouds! Blood was flowing from a garland of human skulls on her neck; human hands encircled and swung from her waist; in her left hand a human skull; on her limbs were streams of blood. Her forehead was adorned with a young moon that touched the extremities of her eyes, lighted up with a bright and fierce flame. It seemed as if Bhoirobi were raising her right hand and calling Kopal-Kundala.

Kopal-Kundala went on with eyes fixed upwards. That form, like a new cloud, went before her along the path of the sky. Now the limbs of the goddess Durga were concealed in the clouds, and again they became clearly visible. Kopal-Kundala fixed her eyes on them, and walked on.

Neither Nobokumar nor the Kapâlik had seen this. Nobokumar's heart was on fire with the poison of the wine. Impatient of Kopal-Kundala's slow footsteps, he said to his companion—

"Kapálik!" The Kapálik said, "What?" "Give me to drink." The Kapálik again gave him wine. Nobokumar said, "Why delay further?" The Kapálik replied, "Why delay further?" Nobokumar called out in a voice of thunder, "Kopal-Kundala!"

Kopal-Kundala heard and was thunder-struck. At this time no one used to call her Kopal-Kundala. She turned her head and stood. Nobokumar and the Kapálik came in front of her. Kopal-Kundala could not at first recognise them. She said, "Who are you? The messengers of death?"

The next moment she recognised them, and said, "No, no, father; have you come to sacrifice me?"

Nobokumar seized Kopal-Kundala's hand with a firm grasp. The Kapálik said in a sweet voice, full of pity, "Child! come with us."

With these words the Kapálik led the way to the burning-ground.

Kopal - Kundala looked towards the sky; where she had seen the terrible form sporting in the sky, she looked there, and saw that the goddess of battle was merrily laughing, and, holding a long trident in her hand, was pointing towards the path the Kapálik had taken. Like one who knew not her fate, Kopal-Kundala without a word followed the Kapálik. Nobokumar went on, firmly grasping her hand as before.

CHAPTER X.

AT THE PLACE OF GHOSTS.

THE moon set. The world was filled with darkness. The Kapálik took Kopal-Kundala to the spot which he had made his place of worship. On the bank of that Ganges was a large expanse of sand, and in front of it another larger expanse of sand. On this sand was the burning-ground. In both places there is a little water at the time of the tide, but none when it has ebbed. Now there was no water. That part of the burning-ground which was close to the river, was very high. To descend into the water, one must fall at once from the high bank into bottomless water. Moreover, the foundations of the bank underneath had been eaten away by the dashing of waves, driven by the ceaseless wind; from time to time pieces of earth would be dislodged and fall into the deep water. There was no light at the place of worship—only a bit of wood was burning, and in its light the burning-ground, dimly seen, looked all the more terrible. At hand were all the requisites for the worship, Hom rites, and sacrifice. The bosom of the broad river lay stretched in the darkness. The wind of the month of Cheitro [1] was speeding along the bosom of the Ganges with terrific force, and the splashing sound caused by the waves dashing against the bank spread to the heavens. On the burning-ground itself could be heard now and again the hideous yells of animals devouring the corpses.

The Kapâlik seated Nobokumar and Kopal-Kundala in a fitting place on a seat of *kus* grass, and commenced his worship in accordance with the rites of the Tantras. At the proper time he ordered Nobokumar to bathe Kopal-Kundala and bring her back. Nobokumar, holding Kopal-Kundala by the hand, led her across the burning-ground to bathe

[1] *Cheitro.* The latter half of March and the first half of April.

her. Bones began to stick in their feet. Nobokumar trod on and broke a funeral-pot full of water. Near it lay a corpse—wretched corpse!—no one had performed its last funeral rites. Both of them touched it with their feet. Kopal-Kundala went round it, Nobokumar trampled it beneath his foot. Wild animals were wandering about in all directions eating the corpses. At the approach of the human beings, they raised loud roars, some came to attack, while others fled away. Kopal-Kundala saw that Nobokumar's hand was trembling. Kopal-Kundala herself was fearless, motionless.

Kopal-Kundala asked, "Husband, are you afraid?" Nobokumar's intoxication from the wine was gradually becoming less. In a very grave voice he replied, "Afraid, Mrinomoi! No."

Kopal-Kundala asked, "Then why do you tremble?"

The voice with which Kopal-Kundala asked this question could only have issued from a woman's throat; such a voice is only possible when a woman's heart melts for another's pain. Who could know that such a voice would issue from Kopal-Kundala's throat on the burning-ground at the time of death?

Nobokumar said, "It is not fear. I cannot cry; through anger at this I am trembling."

Kopal-Kundala asked, "Why should you cry?"

Again that voice!

Nobokumar said, "Why should I cry? Do you wish to know, Mrinomoi? You have never seen and been maddened by beauty" ——

As he spoke Nobokumar's voice was choked with anguish.

"You have never come to tear out your own heart and fling it on the burning-ground." So saying Nobokumar suddenly shrieked and rolled in a fit of weeping at Kopal-Kundala's feet.

"Mrinomoi!—Kopal-Kundala! Save me. Here I am at your feet. Say once that you are not faithless—say that once, and I will raise you to my heart and take you to my home again."

Kopal-Kundala took Nobokumar's hand and lifted him up. She said in a soft voice, "You have never asked me."

When these words were being spoken both had come to and were standing quite on the brink of the water; Kopal-Kundala in front, her back towards the river, the water a single step behind her. The tide had now begun to rise; Kopal-Kundala stood on a ridge, and replied, "You have never asked me."

Nobokumar spoke like a madman, "I am losing my senses, what shall I ask? Speak, Mrinomoi! speak—speak—speak—save me; —come home."

Kopal-Kundala said, "What you have asked, I will tell you. The person whom you saw to-day was Podmaboti. I am not faithless. This is the real truth. But I will not go home again. I have come to lay my body at Bhobani's feet, and I will certainly do so. Husband! Do you go home! I will die! Do not weep for me."

"No, Mrinomoi, no!" shouted Nobokumar, as he stretched out his arms to take Kopal-

Kundala to his heart; but he never found her again. An enormous wave blown up by the Cheitro wind dashed against the bank beneath the spot where Kopal-Kundala was standing, and at that instant a piece of the bank broke and fell into the river with a loud crash, carrying Kopal-Kundala along with it.

Nobokumar heard the sound of the bank breaking, and saw Kopal-Kundala disappear. He instantly leapt into the water after her. Nobokumar was an expert swimmer, and for some time he swam in search of Kopal-Kundala. He did not find her, nor did he himself rise again.

There in that endless Ganges stream, whirled about by the waves that were tossed by the spring wind, Nobokumar and Kopal-Kundala gave up this life.

THE END.